FUR-OCIOUS LUST
BEARS

Love

Molly

FUR-OCIOUS LUST
BEARS

Volume One

New York Times and USA Today Bestselling Author
MILLY TAIDEN

Published By
Latin Goddess Press
New York, NY 10456
http://millytaiden.com
FUR-BIDDEN
FUR-GOTTEN
FUR-GIVEN

ISBN: 1514704730
ISBN 13: 9781514704738

For My Girls
Julie, Teracia, Tonya, Jessica P, Jenn W, Sheri S, and
Nicole V. Thank you for your support.
Love you!

FUR-BIDDEN

ONE

Penelope Medina didn't know how to break the bad news to her best friends. Usually the go-to person to fix anything wrong, she was at a loss how to handle the situation. Karina and Julie chatted animatedly in the too-loud bar they always met at on Friday nights. The scent of smoke, liquor and cheap perfume filled the place. They weren't fond of the dive at first, but it turned into their favorite after-work hangout for the past year.

"So," she started, lifting an apple martini to her lips and taking a sip for courage. "I have something to tell you all."

Her friends stopped chatting about the latest issue at their non-profit and turned to her.

"Uh-oh," Kari said, picking up her cosmopolitan and taking a drink. "You look like you're about to give us bad news."

She was. Dammit! Why did she have to be the one to do it? Jerk-off Dave should be doing it. Not her. She hadn't signed them up for anything.

Dave had, but somehow Penny was the one stuck delivering the bad news.

"Please don't hate me."

"Whoa!" Julie stopped her. "I can already tell I'm not going to like whatever you're going to say, so hang on a sec." She motioned for a refill on her glass of sangria and once that had been taken care of, she gulped the thing down. She then placed it on the table and smacked her lips. "Okay, hit me."

"I swear, Julie, one of these days you're going to fall flat on your face when you stand after doing that a few times. I don't know how you can handle that." Kari laughed.

"Dave signed us up for the bachelorette auction on Sunday," Penny blurted out. Taking a note from Julie, she gulped the rest of her martini. She winced at the burning liquid going down her throat. She had never done that. Not really a drinker, she tended to nuzzle her glass for hours. Tonight called for drastic measures.

"What do you mean he signed *us* up?" Kari screeched.

Yeah. That's the reaction she'd been waiting for. They were three very big girls working for the largest wildlife conservation non-profit in the state. They signed on to work for the company because they loved animals, not to be on a stage getting sold like pieces of meat.

"Penny, I hate to break this to you, but we're shy big girls with bad attitudes," Kari said, her brown eyes wide with surprise.

"Yeah, not just big, we're short. We're not model material. We don't even have the personalities to be good dates." Julie blinked, picking up her glass again and motioning for another refill. "I don't think bitchy goes well with anything."

"I know all of this. Quite frankly, I'm probably more surprised than you two that Dave did that. He knows how we feel about being in the spotlight." She sighed. "But he said we are the best at fundraising and his wife suggested we fill the three empty slots left on the list."

"Weren't all the spots filled?" Kari asked.

"Yeah, but there was a disagreement with some of the volunteers. Apparently, Dave asked them to get clothes they didn't feel comfortable in. He told them to 'sex it up' because 'sex sells' and it would bring the auction lots of money."

"What a douche." Julie shook her head. "So now that leaves us parading on a stage and hoping some poor sap buys us or looking pathetic in front of the entire place, but no pressure, huh?"

None at all.

"We can always quit," Kari suggested, her shoulders slumping. "I don't want to quit though. I love my job."

"Yeah, I do too," Julie said, tossing a long strand of jet-black hair over her shoulder. "Who knew we'd be so good at asking people for money."

Penny curled her fingers over her lap. She hated that Dave had put them in such an uncomfortable position.

Two years ago, Penny had started working at Soaring for Wildlife. Months later, she had met a man she had fallen hard and fast for. The same could be said of her friends. The men were all brothers. But lies, lack of communication, and deception had torn their relationships apart.

Twinges of sadness pinched at her heart. Why did she choose that moment to think of Ethan? Their relationship had lasted only a few months. It'd been filled with lust, romance and half-truths. In the end, that's what killed it. She refused to ask him about things he should have felt comfortable sharing with her. Personal things.

"Look…" She bit her lip, pushing away the memories of Ethan and his blue eyes. "We can say no, but he made it clear our jobs were on the line."

"He's bluffing," Julie said. "We're the best he's got."

"Yeah. Why would he want to get rid of us when we get him more donations between the three of us than everyone in that office, combined?" Kari asked.

The waitress took their empty glasses and brought them fresh drinks. They never had more than one or two, but it appeared tonight was going to be a "walking home" kind of night.

"He's not bluffing." She hated having to give more bad news to her friends. "He showed me three resumes of candidates that come from very well-off backgrounds willing to pull strings to bring the type of donations we have only dreamed of."

"Shit," Julie growled. "This is fucked up. Real fucked up."

"Let me just have five minutes alone with Dave and I will rearrange his face," Kari promised.

"Nobody is getting arrested. We're just going to have to…do it."

Julie made a face of disgust, scrunching her nose and pursing her lips. "Fine. But if neither of you kick Dave in the balls if nobody buys us, I will."

Penny had a plan for that. "That's not going to happen." At least there was something she could do to help them all out in the auction. "I've asked my assistant, Charlie, to buy the three of us. I'm giving him money to at least make it look good."

"I'll double it!" Kari grinned. "I don't want to be sold too cheaply."

"Oh, brother." Julie shook her head.

"Whatever. You know you're going to do the same thing." Kari raised her brows at Julie.

A grin spread over Julie's lips. "Yeah, she's right. Screw Dave. I'll just make my yearly donation work for me."

Great. Now all they needed was for their plan to work, and for Charlie not to leave them hanging.

TWO

Ethan Sinclair turned away from his office window to face the door. His brothers had just walked in. The three bear shifters owned the largest home-building company in the country, Sinclair Building Co..

"Why did you call us?" Rafe asked. Though they were triplets, identical physically, they were completely different in personalities. Ethan was the one behind the contracts. He interfaced with clients and other contractors on a daily basis. Rafe handled builders and materials. Then there was Ash. He was their company's PR man. He helped create their brand and launch Sinclair to the next level. Now they were three of the most powerful men in the United States. All thanks to their exes.

"Penelope, Julie and Karina." He didn't bother warming them up.

"What about them?" Rafe asked, shoving his hands in his pockets and clenching his jaw. He hated talking about Julie.

Ash didn't say a word. He just stood there, his arms folded over his white dress shirt.

"Fine. I can see this is not going to be easy so I'll make it simple. Ash knows we are big donors to the Soaring for Wildlife non-profit. I've made it my business that we donate anonymously every year but the director, Theo, is a friend of mine. He's a lion-shifter who is grateful for our help."

"Get to the point," Rafe growled.

"Fine. The point is that all three of them work at Soaring and we have a chance, if you want to take it, to possibly rectify the situation with them."

Ash lifted a brow. "How?"

"We are the main sponsors for their bachelorette auction this weekend. Theo managed to get the three of them on the roster to be auctioned off for a date. That means you get one chance to ensure your mates listen to you. One chance to change the fuckups from the past." Shit. Saying it out loud sounded even more ominous. He wanted Penny, but she'd hung up on every call he made. She'd ignored his visits and had gone as far as changing her number. Yeah, he'd fucked up big time. This was his chance to get her back. A year without her had been worse than any hell. He'd been waiting for the opportunity to find his way back into her life and he knew that his brothers felt the same way about their women. "Let's just say tonight, they have no choice but to talk to us. I set this up and I ensured Theo would make things happen."

Rafe marched forward, his frame stiffening with every step. "There's no guarantee this will work. They can refuse to see us. Or leave with us."

Ethan grinned. "I have a plan." He pressed a button on his phone and spoke. "Kyle, get in here."

His assistant, Kyle, was a young bear with the ability to smooth talk his way into anything.

Kyle flung the door open and eyed the three men before breaking into a grin. "You told them I'm buying their women?"

Rafe made a deep growling noise in his chest. "Be careful kid. Don't want to break your face. That's the only thing you got going for you."

"I'll have you know, I have the plan all worked out. All you have to do is be at your assigned spot." Kyle puffed out his chest. "You don't pay me the big bucks for nothing."

"Isn't he an intern?" Ash asked.

Ethan laughed. "Yeah."

"Alright," Kyle conceded. "You don't pay me, but once this mission is over, I expect a raise and a bonus and possibly even a vacation."

"You can expect your ass kicked if it doesn't go well," Ash said.

"Such violence!" Kyle grumbled.

"We're fucking bears. What did you expect, sweet talking and roses?" Rafe snapped.

"See that…" Kyle pointed at Rafe while staring at Ethan. "That's why Julie left his ass. I can't promise she'll take him back, Ethan. I'm not a miracle worker. Besides, what if she likes me?"

"Oh, brother," Ash groaned.

Rafe took a step towards Kyle. "I'm gonna—"

"Rafe, stop!" Ethan ordered. "He's going to help and you're going to let him. Now give them both the information they need to be at the right place at the right time, Kyle."

"Fine," Rafe said. "You get to live another day kid."

"You know…" Kyle took slow steps backward. "If I didn't know better I would swear you have not smiled since you and Julie broke up."

"I think you need another plan, Ethan. I'm killing the kid," Rafe said.

Kyle shot out of the room in a heartbeat. He wasn't stupid. Rafe was almost twice his size. All three of them were.

"So what do you think of the plan?" Ethan asked his brothers.

"I think it can work." Ash nodded. "Even if we only get the one chance to talk to them."

"We should come clean already. They didn't deserve the lies." Ethan gripped his pen hard. He wanted to be with Penny. He'd hated letting her go when she'd realized he was keeping things from her. Now, he wasn't going to let another year filled with torture, because he missed her, go by.

"I'm not so sure the truth will be enough with Julie." Rafe marched to the bar at the right side of Ethan's office. He poured three drinks and handed one to each Ash and Ethan.

"Do whatever you need to, to get your woman back, Rafe. Unless you want to keep living without her."

THREE

Penny glanced at the sexiest dress she owned on the backstage mirror. It was a sapphire-blue strapless that showed off her large chest but fell in a cascade of silk, accentuating her curves. It was the first dress she'd bought after leaving Ethan with the thought of dating again, so many months after leaving Ethan. She'd never worn it. Not once. Oh well, it would have to do. It wasn't like she ever went on a date. In fact, she hadn't dated at all since she'd been with him. Ethan had messed her up for all men. His looks. His kisses. He'd been the best for her and she wasn't interested in comparing anyone to him. Besides, she still loved him. There was no way she could honestly feel right about having sex with anyone else when she still wanted the jerk.

Her turn was coming up on the stage. She shoved the curtain to the side, checking out the tables full of couples already getting to know each other. Maybe they'd stop things short and she could be saved.

"There you are!"

She whirled around to face Dave and his wife. Normally, she only disliked Dave, but at that moment she hated his wife, too. Still, she nodded at the woman who gave her what appeared to be a sincere smile. "You look great, Penny."

"Thanks." She managed to get the words out past the lump in her throat. She hated being on-stage. It was why her job was so perfect. All she did was call people. Go to lunch with a single person in charge of charitable contributions. There were no big meetings or public speaking engagements. Her heart started pumping faster than ever.

"You're on, Penny!" she heard someone say.

Holy crap. She couldn't move. Stage fright was going to kill her and she wasn't even on stage yet.

"Come on, darling." Dave's wife, Meredith guided her towards the stage. "Nothing to be afraid of. You're doing something wonderful for charity."

Right. Charity. She needed to keep reminding herself of that or she might throw up. And how sexy would *that* look?

The curtains opened and everyone started clapping. To her right, the Director of Soaring Wildlife stood at a podium and spoke into a mic.

"Now we have the lovely Ms. Penelope Medina."

She glanced out at the crowd but was having a hard time seeing the people with the lights right in her face. She didn't walk up and down like the others had, instead she stood at the same spot, like a petrified animal.

"Ms. Medina is one of our best Development Managers. She likes to dance to eighties freestyle when no one is watching, and she sings in the shower," he read from a paper.

She almost broke her neck jerking around to stare at the director. Who the hell told him that about her? Laughter broke out across the room.

"Ms. Medina is also a fan of Tom and Jerry cartoons and her favorite ice cream is anything with chocolate, vanilla and caramel mixed together. Now let's open up the bid for a night on the town with Ms. Medina. Do I hear fifty dollars?"

Penny couldn't believe someone had divulged her personal information for the stupid auction. The worst part was that she knew it wasn't Dave. He wasn't that familiar with her. She immediately dismissed her friends. She had enough dirt to bury them both. So, who did it?

She heard her assistant, Charlie, yell. "One hundred dollars!"

"I have one hundred dollars from number thirty-five. Do I hear one-fifty?" said the director.

Things were going according to plan. For a second, she thought no other bids were going to come in and smiled, thinking the worst of the night almost over.

"Two hundred dollars," a new voice yelled.

Crap. She squinted into the crowd, trying to find the person bidding against Charlie.

"I have two hundred from the gentleman by the bar," the director said.

Her gaze roamed to the farthest area in the back of the room and she saw a slim young man standing there. She couldn't make out his features well enough to know if she knew him. Fucking hell.

"Two-fifty!" Charlie threw in.

"Three hundred," said the slim guy.

"Three-fifty," yelled Charlie.

She'd only given Charlie five hundred thinking for sure it wouldn't go that high. Now she worried he would lose and soon.

"Four hundred," said the slim guy again, getting a-head of Charlie.

"Five hundred." That was Charlie's highest bid. She held her breath, waiting to see if the other guy would top it.

"I have five hundred from number thirty-five. Do I hear six?" The director encouraged the crowd.

Silence.

"Five hundred dollars going once. Going twice—"

"Fifty thousand dollars," yelled the slim guy.

A murmur rippled through the crowd. She must have heard wrong. The murmur grew louder.

Ah, fuck! She hadn't heard wrong. Why would he pay fifty thousand dollars for dinner with her? What type of person had that kind of money to throw away?

"Fifty thousand going once. Going twice. Sold to the gentleman by the bar for a fifty thousand-dollar donation to Soaring Wildlife. Please meet Ms. Medina by our payment area and we will gladly send you on your way."

FOUR

The crowd went wild cheering for the highest donation of the night so far. Penny's stomach rolled, sending bile shooting up her throat. She could only hope her night got better.

She turned around to go back through the curtain, her hands shaking and her muscles so stiff she swore they'd break. Breathe. She needed to breathe. Spots danced before her eyes.

"Holy shit, Penny!" Julie gasped, clutching her by the shoulders. "You look like you're going to faint."

Penny gasped for air, her lungs burning with panic.

"Breathe, Penny," Kari said softly. "You'll be fine. The guy didn't appear to be more than a kid. Maybe he fell in love at first sight?" She giggled. "Who knows?"

Good. Okay. Why was she freaking out? Oh yeah, the whole time on stage had really messed her up. She took deep breaths, trying to calm the racing in her heart. She wasn't a fan of stages. Or crowds.

Soft as marshmallows, her legs shook with each step she took. "I'm fine. Really, guys. I'm okay."

She cleared her throat and glanced around, looking for the payment area. Where was Dave, that asshole?

"Hey, I wouldn't be so pissed if some young kid bought me," Julie muttered, letting go of Penny's arm. "At least, that would be easier to digest than the looks on some of these old guys' faces."

Penny saw what Julie meant. There were some old men giving bachelorettes lecherous looks and smiling at them like they were pimp daddies. "You're right. This can't be so bad. He's a kid."

A burst of confidence went through her, calming her nerves. This wasn't such a big deal. This was for charity. Why was she getting so worked up? Besides, how many times had she done this before? None. So her worst fears could be unfounded.

"Our next lady up for bid…"

"Crap!" Kari groaned. "My turn. This sucks balls."

"Good luck, girls," Penny said, glancing back at the dreaded stage. "I'll see you all Monday."

"Have fun tonight." Julie smiled. Her sparkling brown eyes filled with concern. "Don't stress so much. This is supposed to be fun all around."

She nodded and marched, with steadier steps, toward the area her friends said was the payment section.

The young man she'd seen from the stage waited for her with a wide smile on his face. He was young, probably early twenties or late teens. "Hi, I'm Kyle."

She shook his hand and immediately felt more at ease. From his short dark hair to his slim frame, the guy didn't give off any jerk vibes. His smile was genuine, which helped her calm down. "Hi. I'm Penelope, but everyone calls me Penny."

"I like that name. Penny. Are you one of the lucky ones?" he asked, the smile growing wider.

She laughed at the question she got from almost everyone. "I like to think so. Did you have something in mind you wanted to do tonight?"

He nodded and offered her his arm. "My car is waiting outside. I think you'll like the place I found for dinner."

She cleared her throat, pushing back the renewed nerves. She didn't normally go anywhere with strangers. Even a young one. Taking his arm, she strolled out of the hall with Kyle. She'd never done a bachelorette auction before so she wasn't sure what the plan was. Thanks to idiot Dave, she hadn't even been filled in on the process.

A shiny black stretch limo sat at the curve of the hotel. Kyle waved at the driver, telling him to stay in place and opened a door for her. She entered the limo and the door closed behind her. A quick glance around made her breath seize in her lungs.

"Ethan?"

The limo sped off and she barely managed to sit properly before she would have fallen on her face. She glanced around, noting that Kyle never got in the limo. Her gaze ate up the man she'd loved but let go.

He'd always worn his brown hair in a shaggy cut that didn't appear to be tamed. His aqua-blue eyes pinned her with a commanding stare. "You look beautiful, Penny."

"What the hell are you doing here?" she screeched in outrage then gasped. "You set this up. You asshole!"

Her chest ached from how good it was to see him and how much it hurt at the same time. She'd missed him so much, but she refused to be with a liar. She didn't care how much he said he loved her.

If he truly did, he wouldn't have lied about some really big things in their relationship, things she expected to know under any circumstance. From the fact he had money down to his species. All of it had been lies.

He leaned forward, his tux shifting with his moves. Christ he had such a big body. She'd always loved that about him. He wasn't all muscle either. He had a well-defined body with strength. It was probably all part of being a bear-shifter. She'd fallen so hard for Ethan. Her mind still couldn't wrap around the fact that he'd kept so much from her. All the while claiming to love her.

"Let me out of this car!" She turned to face the closed partition between them and the driver. Wiggling and sliding down the long curved seat, she was about to knock on the glass when Ethan grabbed her arm, turning her to face him.

"Penny, listen to me."

The limo took a sharp turn and she fell back with Ethan sprawled over her.

"Get off me!" She tried to push him off, but he was too big and strong. He pinned her down until she couldn't move and she wasn't a small woman. She had boundless curves and weight on her body.

She huffed out an angry breath and glared at him. "I don't care how much you paid, I'll have them refund your donation. Now let me out because I am not going anywhere with you."

He held her hands above her head on the seat with one hand and grabbed her chin, forcing her to meet his gaze with the other.

"That's enough!" he roared.

FIVE

She blinked, her heart thundering wildly. She'd never seen him get so angry before.

"Stop acting like a spoiled brat, Penelope." His breath caressed her face and the hint of mint and whiskey floated up her nose. "I wouldn't have had to do this if you would have answered my damn calls. Or opened the door and talked to me."

"You lied to me! I hate liars."

"You don't hate me, babe. You love me," he threw back.

She growled and tried to free herself again. "You are a dick. A big dick."

"I have a big dick. One that's been missing you like crazy, Penny. Stop!" He growled again. "All that moving is only making me want to rip this fucking dress off and fuck you right here right now."

She gasped. "You think I'd let you touch me after what you did?"

He clenched his jaw tight. "What did I do that was so wrong? Keep my finances to myself?"

She rolled her eyes and huffed another growl. "You never told me you were a bear!"

His hand on her face kept her from glancing away from his too-knowing eyes. "You have a problem with me being a shifter?"

"No, you asshole. I have a problem with not being told things that I should know. Like the fact you can turn into a big-ass bear. That's my problem. Get it yet?"

"What the hell does that have to do with anything? If you love me, like you said you did, then you wouldn't care about any of that."

She squirmed again and stopped the moment she felt his erection pressing between her legs. Fucking hell. Now was not the time to get excited he was hard. "I did love you. I didn't care that you were a shifter, but I cared about the lack of trust. You could have told me. It wouldn't have made a difference. I cared about you for you."

"You still love me. Don't fucking try to deny what I can see in your eyes." He rocked his hips between her legs, rubbing his erection right on her clit.

A soft gasp escaped her throat and she bit her lip to keep from moaning. "I can't love a liar."

"I never lied to you." His fierce gaze didn't budge. "I told you I loved you and I was honest."

She glanced down at his lips, her breaths coming in short shallow bursts. "If you loved me, you would have trusted me. Told me about your ass being loaded and a shifter. But you didn't trust me! Get off me!"

He growled and instead of moving like she wanted, he brought his head down and plastered his lips over hers in an angry, soul-sucking kiss that took her breath away. She didn't want to want him. Didn't want to love him. But her body refused to listen. The kiss set off detonations of hunger exploding through her veins. She breathed through his lips, sharing his air and letting him possess her once again. He rubbed his tongue over hers, twirling and sucking and making her lose all control. Pleasure intensified with each swipe of his tongue on her lips. Every nip and nibble sent a stream of wetness down her pussy.

He tore his lips from hers and inhaled a short, harsh breath. "You want me."

She licked her lips, still staring at his too-sexy mouth and lied. "I don't."

"You're so fucking wet for me, Penny."

"Bullshit. You have a good imagination." She refused to admit defeat. She didn't care how much her body burned for the bear. She wouldn't give in to her hormones.

"Bullshit?" He lowered his head again, sucking on her chin and licking her jaw. "I know I make you wet. I bet if I shove my hand between your legs you'll be fucking soaked."

She swallowed back a whimper. Lord have mercy on her soul. "You're delusional. I don't want you."

"You can lie to yourself, but you can't lie to me. Your body aches for me to get inside you. Your pussy throbs for a taste of my cock."

Holy shit. Hearing him say it only made her wetter. "I don't know what you're talking about. I know how to control myself."

"You're a piece of work. You lay there, wet and horny as fuck, wanting me to fuck you every way possible and you refuse to admit it."

She licked her lips and raised her brows. "Let me out of this car. I don't negotiate with liars."

"I'm not a liar!" He took her mouth again, this time even harder than before. The sound of material tearing resonated in the back of her mind, but the way he fucked her mouth with his tongue pushed it all away. She gave in, just a little, and kissed him as hard as he kissed her. A loud rumble sounded from his chest, making her entire body vibrate.

Then his mouth was on her neck, sucking, biting, driving her crazy with each touch. She couldn't look down; he still had a hand on her face, holding it in place. It took a second to realize he wasn't holding her hands above her head any longer. He'd released them and she'd kept them up there on her own.

She gripped his hair in her fist. At first, to pull him away, but the moment his lips sucked on her nipple it changed to keep him there. She hated how badly she wanted him. It had always been like this between them. Hot. Rough. Dangerous.

Her temperature shot to the moon when he nipped at her breast. It was so good. So right. He slid his hand down her body and between her legs, yanking at the material of her panties. The bite of pain from the pull of the silk didn't faze her. She ignored that and opened wide. Maybe for this one time she could take what he offered. A quick bout of pleasure before she sent him away from her. There wasn't going to be a relationship between them again. But this, sex, she could do.

He groaned on her breast and released her nipple. He pressed his palm on her pussy, pushing his fingers into her entrance. "Fuck, Penny. I told you you'd be wet."

She gulped and tried to push her need for more of his touch away. "I'm not."

His face came into view. The angry frown and the way he pressed his lips into a thin line made her heart flip-flop. "Now who's the liar?" He spread her pussy lips wide open and flicked a finger on her clit. "You don't want to want me, but you do. You're fucking visualizing me up in your pussy. Deny it all you want, but my cock is the only one that does this to you. I make you slick. I make you hot. I make you come." His finger circled the sensitive nub and she moaned. "Say it. Say you want me to fuck you."

"I—"

He fingered her pussy, drawing out a low moan from her. "Say you want my dick inside you. You know you do. You've been thinking about it since the last time I fucked you."

She gasped, closing her eyes and then opening them again to his piercing gaze. "Ethan…"

"That's it baby," he said when she grew slicker. "You remember that last time. It was kind of like this. In a limo. Remember how I ate your pussy until you gushed on my face?"

Oh, good god how could she ever forget that. It had been unreal. She nodded, her body trying to take the tenuous control out of her grasp.

"You wet my face with your juices and then I kissed you. You tasted yourself on my mouth and begged me to fuck you. Remember that, sweetheart? Remember my cock deep in your pussy?" He pushed two fingers into her and drew them out slowly. "You moaning how much you liked it. Your nails digging my back and your legs spread wide so I could go deeper and deeper." His fingers went in and out of her faster, picking up speed with his words. "I remember. Maybe it's time I reminded you how much your pussy likes my cock sliding in and out of you. How much you love me coming inside you, leaving you sticky and wet and then eating you out all over again."

Fucking hell! Why did he do that to her? "Ethan, I can't—"

He brushed his lips lightly over hers. "Say it. You want to. I know because I haven't wanted another like I want you. I haven't been with anyone since you. And there will not be any others. It's just you."

She didn't know if he was lying or telling the truth, but those words did something to her. It opened the door she'd shut a year ago and emotions poured out of her like a glass of wine overflowing. "Please." She swallowed. "I've missed you."

That's all it took. He pushed the frothy skirt out of the way and unzipped. His gaze was stuck to hers. There was no need for further workup or words. All she wanted was him. Inside her. Taking her. Being hers. He pushed the head of his cock into her slick channel with a single-minded thrust and didn't stop until he was balls deep inside her, until she was choking for a breath from her body was trying to adjust to being taken after almost a year without him.

"Fuck, baby. You're still just as perfect as before." He pulled his hips back and pressed forward with determined drives.

She clawed at his suit jacket, wishing the damn thing was off him, but not wanting to stop him for anything. He fucked her the way she loved. Hard. Fast. Deep. So deep. Until they were pelvis to pelvis with no space between them.

"Yes…" she moaned.

The limo hit a bump and his thrust felt deeper. She didn't care that his hand was still on her neck, holding her in place. She only focused on the pleasure of his body going in and out of hers. Tension mounted inside her, curling at the pit of her belly into a ball, ready to unfurl at any second.

"Lord, you feel good." He sucked on the corner of her mouth, biting his way down to her neck. "Your pussy's so tight. So wet. I've been dreaming of being inside you again for the past year." He drew circles over her skin with his tongue. "Dreams of coming in your pussy. In your mouth. Taking you every way. You'd let me. You'd want me to fuck you hard and rough until your legs were useless."

She moaned, her lungs burning from the lack of air. She visualized him doing even more to her. Just like he had in the past. "Yes, I would let you."

"I know," he groaned, his words coming out choppy and strained. "You loved it when I fucked you from behind and yanked on your gorgeous hair. And when I slapped your ass. Didn't you, Penny?"

She did. Dammit all to hell she did! She'd never wanted a man to do any of that to her until Ethan. He'd opened her up to want things she'd never thought sexy. He'd done stuff to her she hadn't even thought of. "I—"

"Don't deny it now, love," he rumbled. "I've licked and fucked you in every way possible. I've loved watching you play with yourself when you sucked my dick. Fuck! That was so sexy." He thrust harder, his moves almost losing their precision.

"Ethan," she gasped. Her muscles stiffened. She was so close. So close to jumping off the cliff and diving into a whirlpool of pleasure. "I'm so…"

"I got you, beautiful." He lowered his head to her chest and bit down on her nipple. Sucking and biting hard and fucking her with the same aggression did the trick. His pelvis rubbed on her clit, adding just the right amount of friction to push her over the edge and send her soaring.

She screamed, clutching on-to his jacket and taking a pounding from his cock at the same time her pussy contracted around him with her orgasm. She slid up and down on the leather seat, her back slick with sweat. Then he stiffened, groaning and pumping with a speed she knew meant he was closing in on his own release. Once. Twice. He stopped, bit harder on her tit and groaned. His cock pulsed in her pussy, filling her with his seed.

SIX

Ethan held the woman he'd fallen for like a stone in his arms. Two years ago, he'd broken all the rules his family had lived with and started dating Penny. She was a human, unlike any of the females in his clan. At first, he'd chosen not to tell her about his shifter status because he wasn't sure how she'd react. Not that he hadn't slept with human females, but she was different. She was the one. The more time he spent with her, the more he realized he didn't want her to leave him. Unlike him and his brothers, she'd been raised dirt poor with almost nothing to her name.

Thinking of her history and how she'd come out of it, the struggle she'd endured to become something in a family of nothing, tugged at his heart. He'd been trying to figure out how to tell her of his wealth without sounding full of himself. Or without making her feel like she wasn't good enough for him.

What ended up happening, was that she'd found out through word of mouth, something he hadn't expected. He could almost hear her brain working, trying to decide what to do about him. About them. Only this time, he wouldn't let her just close him out and push him away because she felt deceived. He'd never actually lied to her. He'd gone as far as baring his soul so she could see he loved her. Nothing had worked.

"Ethan." She shifted, leaving his arms, holding with one hand the pieces of what used to be her dress up to her chest. She slipped shaky fingers through her curls, pushing the long, dark strands away from her face. "We need to talk."

He didn't dare smile, though he wanted to, at the mussed-up hair and smeared make-up. God, she was so fucking beautiful. Even like this: angry, confused and a mess, he wanted her again. She could be wearing a box and he'd want her. There was no taming the desire he felt for her. Would always feel for her.

He handed her his shirt, hoping she'd feel more comfortable wearing that, but also for his own peace of mind. There was no way in hell he'd be able to sit there and talk to her when all he wanted to do was tear the fabric away and fuck her until he came inside her at least three more times. He wanted to pound her hard, fucking her until he couldn't go on, draining himself in her. The bear demanded he reclaim her body.

"I never lied to you," he said. Though saying the words he'd repeated to her should be easy, it still bothered him that she had honestly believed him capable of deceit. He might not have told her about his bear or his money, but he never lied about his feeling for her. Ever.

"Look." She cleared her throat, her gaze sweeping down his naked torso and his pants' open fly. "I don't know if I could trust you after that."

He stayed where he was. The bear snarled and huffed, wanting to get her to understand she belonged with him. "You love me."

She narrowed her eyes, pursed her lips and took a slow breath. "Love is not the issue here. Trust is."

"I never lied about my feeling for you. I love you. I have since the first moment I saw you. I love everything about you." He stared her down, holding her gaze captive and willing her to believe him. "I love your attitude. I love your sexy-as-hell body. All those curves make me fucking crazy. I love your generosity in wanting to work saving wild life. I love the fact that you have been offered jobs that pay more and refuse them to stay at a non-profit."

Her eyes widened. "Who told you about that?"

He shrugged. "I know everything about you, love. I've never for a second stopped thinking about you. About bringing you back to where you belong, with me."

She bit her lip and frowned. "Why didn't you tell me about your money? Or the fact you were a shifter?"

"You were so open about having nothing most of your life. I hated that I'd grown up with none of those problems. I tried to not sound like a jackass by flaunting money or suggesting things that would make you uncomfortable."

"I don't understand."

He smiled. He'd paid attention to her. He'd seen her reaction when he'd given her some inexpensive gifts and how she'd almost refused them. "I had to stop myself from giving you everything I saw, because you made it clear that buying you things was not the way to get your attention."

She nodded. "It's not. I don't need material things. I've done without them and can continue to. That's not what makes me happy."

He took a deep breath, his stomach burning from the words that were ready to spill. "I was scared to lose you. I thought if you knew I had money, you'd push me away."

"I—"

36

"I shouldn't have kept that from you. I thought that if you didn't find out until later on, things would be easier for you to get used to."

"I loved you, Ethan. I would have understood. Just because I didn't have money doesn't mean I'd begrudge you yours. That's selfish and wrong."

He laughed dryly. "I see that now."

"What about the other thing? Why not explain to me about your bear? Did you think I didn't know about shifters?"

"No. It wasn't that. Many women get caught up in the idea of being with a shifter and they either freak out, thinking we're going to somehow hurt them, or they start asking for strange things."

"Again. You didn't trust me enough to tell me. You thought I would be like the others."

"At first I didn't know you well enough."

"But after?"

"I was wrong. I...I should have told you but by then, you were entrenched in my heart. In my blood. I couldn't imagine you not being in my life." He opened himself up, ready for the possibility of her rejection but still willing to let her know how he felt. "You're the first woman I have cared enough about that it worried me what you thought."

"Take me home, Ethan. I need to think." She bit her lip and glanced away. "I'm not saying I don't want to see you again. I just need to figure out if I can be in a relationship with you and trust you. If I can't, then there is no saying yes to you. It would be a waste of both our time. The last thing either one of us needs is a relationship with no trust."

He nodded, willing to give her the time and space she needed. Only he wasn't just going to go away. He wasn't going to disappear into the night and pretend he didn't love her, that he didn't want her. A year without her had been hell and he wasn't going to go through another.

He pressed the intercom button and gave the driver her address. His mind worked out the plans for getting her back in his life again. Money was no longer an issue; he'd use whatever means necessary to show her he loved her, to show her how much he cared.

When they reached her house, he got out of the limo and helped her to her front door. She wrapped his shirt around her, so big it looked like a dress on her.

She opened her door and turned to face him, her eyes filled with confusion. "Thank you for bringing me back. And for the donation."

He nodded, watching her get ready to close the door on him. The bear didn't want to let go just yet.

He shoved his foot in the door and pushed it wide enough to fit his frame. She opened her mouth to say something but he hooked a hand around her neck and pulled her to him. He brought his lips down over hers. The sound of her soft moan drove the beast forward.

A rumble sounded in his chest. He yanked the bear back, focusing his energy on the taming of her lips. The sweet taste of her appeased some of his hunger, but not enough. The soft whimpers of pleasure turned his hard cock concrete stiff. He needed inside her again. Fuck fuck fuck! All he wanted was to lay her down and eat her pussy and drive his cock so deep her pussy would clasp around him. She'd moan and offer her tits to him and he'd take her all fucking night. That's what he wanted. For the rest of his damn life.

He yanked away from the temptation she'd become and met her stunned gaze. He licked his lips, taking in the lingering flavor. How he wanted to lick her smooth caramel skin all over, to kiss his way down her spine until he reached her ass and dipped his tongue between her cheeks. She puffed out a breath and tortured her bottom lip with her teeth.

"Don't tempt me anymore," he growled. "All I want to do right now is fuck you against this door."

Her brows rose and her lips lifted in a small grin. "I don't think you sound like someone who has his beast under control."

He glanced at the slightly open neckline of his shirt, showing off her mouth-watering tits. "My beast wants to fuck you. I want to fuck you. And to be honest with you, I could probably spend the rest of my life with you, in a bed, your legs spread wide, sating my hunger for you."

She glanced over his shoulder. "Let me think, Ethan."

"You've had a year to think, Penny. It's my turn to make you mine again."

She gulped and the scent of her arousal tickled his bear. She was going to drive him fucking crazy. He could tell she liked that he was half out of his mind wanting her. His brother Rafe was right, women were a lot of work. He thought about Penny under him, screaming his name and decided the reward of having her back was worth it though.

He turned around and marched to the limo, the bear snapping at his heels and begging to be let loose.

SEVEN

Ethan's instinct was to grab the largest bouquet of tulips he could find. He knew those were Penny's favorite, and he planned to make sure she knew he was going to get her back. It wasn't a matter of if; it was a matter of when. She would be his again. Fuck that, she was his, she just needed to remember.

He knew it was early and she'd probably be at home, puttering around like she tended to do on a Saturday morning when she didn't have to go anywhere. He'd found out all about her schedule and knew this was the day she stayed home and relaxed.

He rung her bell and waited, excitement roaring inside him in the form of an antsy bear. He wanted to see her. If it were up to his animal, he'd never be away from her. Though most of his clan liked to live solitary lives, when they found a mate, there was no being away from them. Ethan had seen the change in himself the moment he met Penny. There were no longer thoughts of being away from the world.

Everything revolved around her and making her happy. For months, that's exactly how it had gone.

The door swung open and Penny stood in doorway, her nose red and her eyes watery.

"What happened? You looked fine last night." He marched inside, ignoring the fact she hadn't invited him in.

"Gee, thanks." She sniffled and sneezed. "I've been working hard and had the sniffles recently. It's turned into a full-blown cold."

Panic coursed through him, seizing his ability to breathe. Penny had never gotten sick when they were together before. He wanted to make her feel better. He had to do something to help her.

He shoved the flowers into her hands. "What can I get you?"

She glanced down at the bouquet of tulips and then lifted her shiny gaze to his. "These are so beautiful."

"Never mind the flowers." He urged her toward the sofa, dropping his cell phone on the coffee table in front of her. "Lay down."

She blinked up at him, her stunned gaze going from the flowers to him. "I'm not going to fall over because I have a cold. What are you doing here anyway?"

He took the flowers out of her hands and headed for her kitchen. He'd learned the layout well enough back when they'd dated. He searched her cupboards until he found an empty glass vase and half-filled it with water before arranging the flowers. "I wanted to ask if you wanted to go for breakfast."

She sneezed again. He brought the vase to the coffee table and put them where she could look at the tulips.

"I don't really feel like going out." She coughed. "I'm kind of tired and it was a long week at work."

He nodded and went back to the kitchen. "Just lay there. I'll make you something to eat. Does an omelet sound okay or do you want something else?"

"You cook?" she asked, her voice loud with surprise.

He'd never actually done any cooking in the past when they'd been together, but he knew how to take care of basic things like breakfast and sandwiches. Anything more complicated than that and he'd need the takeout menu.

He checked her fridge and frowned. "You don't have anything in here."

"Yeah," she sighed. "I was supposed to go food shopping today."

Penny sneezed again. She'd felt run down the previous day and should have known the cold was coming, but with everything that went on at the stupid bachelorette auction, she'd ignored her body's warning signs.

She peeked over the back of the sofa to the kitchen. Ethan searched through her fridge. He shut the door and returned to the living room. "I'm going to get some things to make breakfast. Got any requests?"

She nodded. "There's this bakery down the road that makes amazing croissants."

"I know which one. I used to get honey buns there. They're great." He marched out of the house, leaving her all kinds of confused.

Ethan, this Ethan, was so…different. The same, but different. There hadn't been this much catering to her when they'd been together before. In the past she'd felt like he'd been tiptoeing around her, almost afraid to say or do something to upset her.

The ringing of a cell phone caught her attention. She glanced at the coffee table. It was his phone. She shouldn't answer it, but curiosity had her staring at the screen. The name displayed didn't look familiar. She wouldn't answer. That was wrong and totally inappropriate. Besides, if it were her phone? She wouldn't want anyone answering her calls. The

44

ringing stopped and the cell phone vibrated in her hand. She glanced down at the screen when a text message appeared.

Have you figured out what to do
about your wife?

She blinked and re-read the message. Wife? Wife? Wife! Anger flourished inside her, growing into a massive monster looking for destruction. She took deep breaths and tried to ignore the pain. Ethan, married? Could it be? But why pursue her then? She shook her head and pushed the flood of emotions back. This could all be a misunderstanding. Ethan wasn't a cheater. Not that she was in a relationship with him, but she knew that much about him. She knew he wouldn't do that.

After ten minutes of pacing the living room until she couldn't stand her own inability to shut out the angry words springing to mind, she heard her door open.

"Sorry I took so long, I got the croissants and some other things to make breakfast," he said carrying large bags toward the kitchen.

"Your phone was ringing while you were gone. You forgot it on my table," she said, bringing it to the kitchen and handing it to him. Then she stood there, watching his face as he glanced at the screen, looking for any sign of guilt or fear.

He grinned and lifted his gaze from the phone. "Guess you're wondering about the text, huh?"

She shrugged as if it were no big deal. Like she wasn't visualizing ways to smash the phone on his head. "Oh? What message?"

He laughed and yanked her by her robe into his arms. "Will you believe me if I tell you I'm not married and you're the only woman I want?"

She thought about it for a second before replying. "Yes."

He hugged her tight and brushed his lips over her forehead. "I'm not married, I swear."

"I believe you. But why did you get a message asking about your wife?"

He let go of her and started taking food out of the bags. "That's my cousin Terry. She likes joking around because she knows you are the only woman I ever wanted for a wife. She'd heard about what I was doing at the auction and this was her way of asking how things went. When I met you, I told her you were going to be my wife, so she's been referring to you that way since then."

She frowned. "Wait, you told her I was going to be your wife since you met me?"

He nodded, placing the makings for breakfast on the counter. "Yes. From the very first day I knew you were it for me."

46

She gulped back the knot in her throat and sniffled. Stupid runny nose. Yeah, blame that and not the abundance of emotions filling her heart. "You…you never told me that."

He cupped her face with both hands; his honest gaze warmed her to the bone. "I didn't know how much I could give you back then. I didn't want to scare you. Bears know their mates. We live for them and don't ever want them away from us. That's the animal in me. The man loves the beauty he saw in you. The sweetness. The unselfishness. You're everything I could have asked for in a woman, Penny. Everything and more."

He'd really brought out the big guns. She wasn't sure if it was the fact that she had a cold or that she'd spent the entire night rehashing her feelings for Ethan, but she couldn't turn away from him. There was no leaving and not without giving them a second chance.

"Now, go lay down and let me pamper you."

EIGHT

She went back to the sofa and lay there with a throw over her. After dozing for a few minutes, she woke to the scent of food. She sat up when he came around the sofa with a tray. He put the tray on the table. He passed her a mug of tea with honey and lemon, and a plate of food.

"Wow, this looks so good. You didn't have to."

He winked. "Don't say that until you've tried it. You might be saying it for real after you eat."

She picked up a fork and ate, watching him drink a cup of coffee. The rest of the day went on like that, with him bringing things to her in bed and finally running a bath so she could lay down feeling refreshed. She took some cold medicine and woke up hours later to find him lying next to her. The idea of him and her again didn't bring on the fear and distress it once had. She'd been stupid and naïve. She should have trusted her instincts when it came to him.

He'd offered nothing but happiness and she'd blown it the moment she found out something he

48

hadn't told her. Instead of getting angry, what she should have done was try to figure out why he'd felt the need to keep things from her. That would have saved her being away from her bear for a year: a year of loneliness and heartache.

She glanced at his face. Even in sleep he looked ready to break something. Her gaze caressed the beard growth on his chin. She continued letting her vision travel down. His chest rose and fell with smooth breaths. At the beginning of their relationship, she'd refused to believe she'd fallen for him so quickly. But she had.

After meeting him at a wild life conservation dinner, he didn't have to work too hard at getting her into his bed. From the moment their gazes clashed, lust and need exploded inside her. He'd done that. Taken her from a woman who never slept with a guy on a first date, to one who moved in with him a week later.

The passion between them hadn't dimmed the entire time they'd been together. Looking at him now, her body heating from just gazing at him, she knew the need for him would never go away. She moved down to his waist, unbuckled his jeans and shoved her hand in to grasp his cock, pumping him in her grip.

His eyes snapped open and his hand caught her wrist. "What are you doing?"

She grinned, her body humming with need. "If you have to ask, then I must not be doing something right."

He let go of her hand and she tugged his jeans down, until his erection was freed from the confines of the denim. She leaned forward and circled her tongue on the head of his cock, moaning at the salty taste of his smooth, velvety flesh.

She closed her eyes, her focus solely on him, making this moment good for both of them. With one hand, she pumped his shaft while pushing him further down her throat. He sucked in his abs with every scratch she did made down his chest.

He groaned, slid a fist into her hair and held on to a chunk. "That's fucking perfect, baby. I love how you suck my cock." He pushed her head toward his pelvis. "Those sexy sounds you make every time you suck are driving me crazy."

She knew what sounds he referred to. It was the saliva in her mouth combined with every slide of her lips over his slick dick. She scraped her nails on his abs with each hard suck.

"Take my cock, baby. Yeah," he grunted. "Fucking hell your mouth is so good. I can't fucking think straight."

She continued bobbing her head up and down his cock, jerking him with her hand. He tugged on the hair he had in his grip and let out a slow breath. "Come here. I want to taste that sweet honey coating your pussy."

She let go of his cock and sat back, taking off the tank top and short she'd had on. He didn't give her a second. He shoved her on to her back and curled his arms around her thighs, pushing her legs wide open and taking an immediate lick of her pussy. She squealed, her back coming off the bed and her fingers darting into his hair, to hold him in place.

"Oh, Ethan."

He shoved his tongue into her pussy, licking and suckling and making slurping noises she found so damn sexy. He kissed her inner thigh and then bit her. "I love your taste. I could live right here, fucking this sweet pussy with my tongue."

She opened her mouth and the only thing that came out was a loud moan. He lay his tongue flat on her pussy and swiped it up and down. Then, when she was squirming and rocking her hips hard on his face, he sucked her clit into his mouth, at first bypassing it with his tongue. Every small swipe made her muscles tense harder, until her legs were shaking and she was taking choppy breaths.

"Ethan, please."

He chuckled and licked another circle around her clit. "I fucking love you like this. Wet. Hungry. Ready to come all over my face."

"Stop the torture," she gasped.

Quick as lightning, he struck. He nibbled on her aching clit and sucked her hard. Her body shook as a wave of pleasure drained the tension away, bathing her in a sea of bliss.

She gasped, moaned and let her body do its own thing. She'd yet to catch a breath when he pushed his cock into her, her pussy walls still fluttering around him from her orgasm. He slid right in, taking her in a single drive.

He held her face in his hands, meeting her gaze with a tender one of his own. "I love you, Penny."

She hadn't wanted to think about love just yet, but there was no denying her feelings. She'd never stopped loving her bear.

"I love you too."

He pulled his hips back and drove forth, grunting with the punishing drive.

She whimpered, raking her nails over his large shoulders.

"I love your smile." He propelled back and pushed hard again. "I love every gorgeous curve on you. And don't you dare debate with me about how big you are. You're the perfect size for me."

She grinned. "I'm still really big."

"I like big. I love curves. Yours feel fucking amazing when I'm in you." He stroked his lips over hers. "More than anything, I don't want you to ever feel like I'm being dishonest or keeping things from you. I'll tell you everything. All I am is yours. All I own is yours." He kissed her harder, flirting his tongue over hers and then cutting the kiss short right when she opened up for more. "I don't feel whole unless you're with me."

"Please," she mumbled. "You have to move faster. I'm so close."

He thrust deeper. Every plunge pushed her to moan louder. To take sharper breaths. Everything but the feel of him possessing her body blurred. Nothing else mattered.

He gripped her hip with a hand, his fingers biting deep into her flesh. He rolled his own and she saw stars. His cock rubbed against an area that sent her soaring. The scream that rolled out of her caught her unawares. Her fingers turned stiff from how hard she clung to his shoulders. Her pussy clamped tight around his cock as pleasure washed over her, liquefying her bones and muscles.

His thrust turned jerky, every move slowed until he held stiff above her. Then he groaned, his cock filling her pussy with his cum. She gulped, trying to catch a breath. He flipped on his side, pulling her to lay sprawled half-on half-off him.

It took long minutes before either could move and when one did, it was her. She lifted her head from his chest to stare deep into his eyes.

"I love you. I don't want to be separated any longer."

"Thank fuck, baby. I don't think I could have survived it," he said, running his fingers over the back of her head. "I meant what I said. I won't ever keep anything from you again. You're the only woman I have ever loved and I don't ever want you to feel like I've deceived you in any way."

She smiled and laid her head back on his chest. "Good. Next time I won't be as nice."

"There won't be a next time. There's a forever and that's you and me, babe."

She liked the sound of that. Forever with her bear.

FUR-GOTTEN

ONE

Karina Roma went through every dress in her closet with disgust. She hated dressing up. What she should do was show up at that stupid auction in a pair of sweats and some flip-flops. That would show Dave to stop assuming his employees were willing to do anything for his lazy, annoying ass.

Her doorbell rang, and she threw a glare at the clothes piled on her bed. There were so many different outfits; she couldn't see her pretty, purple bedspread.

She yanked the door open with a lot more force than necessary, the wood thumping loudly against the wall when she let go. It was her sister, Jessie.

"What's going on? I got your voicemail, and all I heard was screeching, mumbling, and cussing," Jessie said, shoving the door open and marching past Kari.

"Dave, my boss, is an asshole."

"I thought we'd come to that conclusion a long time ago? Didn't he cancel your last day off because he wanted to go golfing and needed you to sit there and entertain some donors?"

Kari tossed the long strands of hair falling out of her ponytail over her shoulder and stomped toward her bedroom, Jessie following close behind. "He went too far this time. He signed us up for a bachelorette auction."

Like Kari, Jessie was a big girl herself, except Jessie was a lot more shy and subdued. Kari was known for speaking her mind. It was the reason she got along so well with her best friends, Julie and Penny. At one point, the three had dated triplets. Even more astounding was the fact they'd never confused the identical men. Kari knew Ash from his brothers every time. He was the one dressed in the suits that impressed and who wore a shorter, spikier haircut. There was always a hint of flirtiness with Ash that his brothers didn't have. He liked to laugh a lot and do things she'd never considered.

"Okay, so this auction, it's worrying you because…"

"I don't like people!"

Jessie chortled. "Yeah, that much is obvious. But why is it really bothering you?"

"I dislike the idea that he has put us in a position to be seen like leftovers."

"Excuse me?" Jessie gasped. "What do you mean leftovers?"

"Look. I get it. I'm a big girl, and I'm more than fine with that. I've lived in this body my whole life, and I'm happy with it. What I don't appreciate is for him to get seven other sexed-up women and have the three of us follow behind like the ones nobody wants."

"Ahhhh…" Jessie shoved clothes to the side so she could make a spot to sit on the bed. "I get it. But it doesn't have to be that way. You are gorgeous in your own way."

"Yes, I know this." Not that she was full of herself or anything, she just liked to believe her curves rocked. She didn't want to be skinny or any other way than what she was. "But he put us in the end like we're his afterthoughts. That's the part that pisses me off."

"Did you want to go first?"

"Hell no!"

Jessie laughed again. "You are one confused woman."

She wasn't. She understood herself. When she'd dated Ash, she'd had too many run-ins with the willowy type of women he dealt with in his position at his family's company. The comments and sneers she'd listened to had pushed her past the ability to be polite. On more than one occasion, she'd found herself having to defend her shape to women who said she was too fat to be with such a handsome man.

Ash had been great back then. He'd always stepped up to cut down anyone who tried to make her feel low. What ended their relationship was his constant traveling. She'd let a lot of things slide, but when he was not around for weeks, sometimes months, she didn't see a point in being with him any longer. His schedule took him away from her for crazy lengths of time. He called, but that didn't feel like enough. Not to her. She'd been ready to move her work hours around to be with him, and seeing him not make the same effort only drove the point home that she needed to cut things off.

"So why am I here?" Jessie asked, breaking through her memories. "It appears a tornado took hold of your room." She snickered. "And you say I'm the pig in the family."

"You are the pig, Jessie. You don't clean, you don't cook, and you don't do laundry."

"Hey, paying other people to do all that doesn't make me a pig. It just makes it so that I can enjoy my time doing things that I want to do."

"Just help me find a dress," Kari snapped. "And stop smiling. I'm going to make sure your ass is signed up to next year's auction. See how you like it."

"You need to embrace your time on the stage, hermana. Think of it this way: all those men will get a chance to see you dressed up and looking even hotter than usual."

Kari rubbed her eye. Stupid contacts were bugging her again. It felt like a bucket of sand had been dropped in her eyes. "Look, pick a dress. I'm going to take a shower and take these contacts off before I look like I smoked something to help me relax."

Jessie giggled and tossed her a blue top. "Maybe you do need something to make you relax. Want a glass of wine?"

"Yeah, and while you're at it, make yourself something to eat. I'm too nervous to think of food," she said, heading to the shower.

TWO

Kari entered the nicest hotel in the city with a pep to her step. She looked damn good, and she knew it. Her sapphire-blue dress made her mocha skin shine. Jessie had helped her blow dry and curl her hair into long, fluffy curls that fell around her shoulders. Even her makeup had come out like it had been expertly applied. She had to admit she felt sexy.

Her golden sandals clicked on the marble floor in the lobby, drawing everyone's attention. A few men stopped to stare, and she grinned and winked. What the hell? She felt good. The auction was part of the annual ball for her job. She knew that it would only be a few minutes of her time onstage, but she'd sure as hell make them count. A new wave of self-assurance swept through her.

The ballroom was crowded with women in all kinds of gowns and men wearing tuxes. She searched the area for her two friends. Julie, in a gorgeous, body-hugging silver gown waved as she strode her way.

"Oooh, Kari, you look hot."

"Um, have you looked in a mirror lately? That dress is stunning."

Julie glanced down at her dress with a cheeky grin. "I had nothing to wear, so I ended up going shopping. Can I just say, I have enough ball gowns to go to all the proms in the city if the need arises."

Kari shook her head, grinning at Julie's lack of control when it came to shopping. She loved to buy things. That was her biggest weakness. When it came to shoes, dresses, and bags, Julie had a collection neither Kari nor Penny could compete with.

"Hey, guys," Penny said, walking up to them.

"Hey, yourself, stranger." Kari grinned. "Looking hot, Ms. Medina."

"Yeah," Penny snorted. "Tell that to these heels. They're killing my feet."

"That's why I went with these." Kari lifted the hem of her dress and showed off her two-and-a-half-inch sandals. "There's going to be no limping for me tonight with sky-high heels." She glanced at Julie's peeking toes. "How many inches are you wearing tonight?"

Julie lifted the hem of her dress, and her spiked sandals came into view. "Only three inches."

"Those look bigger than three inches," Kari said.

"They might be. Unlike men, I don't estimate up," Julie said, as she accepted the champagne flute the waiter passing by handed her.

"You are so bad." Penny laughed. "Ah shit. The stupid auction is starting. I wish someone would just donate a shit ton of money and make this all be over with."

"Hey, you never know," Kari mused. "Maybe one of us will get the highest bid. Wouldn't that just beat all?"

Julie blew a raspberry. "And pigs can fly."

* * *

Kari stared as Penny marched stiffly off to meet her young date. She'd just gotten the highest bid of the night. She wasn't expecting a fifty-thousand-dollar bid for her time, but she'd be happy to get a good donation for the company.

She marched up to the stage and waited until her name was called out.

"Next up is Ms. Karina Roma. Ms. Roma loves to bake. Her specialty is a chocolate cake that will make a man drop to his knees and beg."

The smile she'd pasted on her face as she walked onto the stage faltered for a second. Who told him she liked to bake? Nobody knew that but Jessie.

Not even Julie and Penny knew she baked. It was something she did when she was stressed—a way to relax and eat her favorite food: chocolate.

"Ms. Roma enjoys doing exhilarating sports, like bungee jumping and sky diving."

Say what? Okay, that they could have gotten from her friends, but why would he mention it?

She stopped in the center of the stage and tried to keep the frown pushing its way to her face at bay. She glanced around the tables, looking for Penny's assistant, Charlie. He waved at her from the left side of the bar, and she relaxed. Everything was going to be fine. She'd given up her last month's paycheck to ensure she got 'bought' at a decent price. She wasn't rich, but she could afford it. She was careful with her money and didn't lead an extravagant lifestyle, so it was okay to do this one time.

"Do I hear five hundred dollars for Ms. Roma?"

Charlie raised his number. "Five hundred and fifty."

Then, out of nowhere, a second person on the other side of the bar raised his number. No! What the hell was that guy doing?

"Six hundred dollars," said the guy she didn't know.

"Eight hundred dollars," Charlie countered.

"One thousand dollars," the man replied.

"Looks like Ms. Roma is one hot candidate." The director chuckled. "Do I hear one thousand two hundred?"

"Fifteen hundred dollars," Charlie yelled.

"Three thousand dollars," said the stranger.

Kari's gaze jerked back and forth between both men as if she were watching a ping-pong match.

"Five thousand dollars," Charlie said. That was it. He'd reached her highest bid. That was a full month's pay and some of her savings. All so she wouldn't be sold at the lowest bid.

The room held still in utter silence.

"Do I hear six thousand?"

Silence.

"I have five thousand dollars going once... going twice," the director said, and just as she started letting out an anxious breath, the other man raised his number, and she knew she'd been outbid.

"One hundred thousand dollars."

A wave of gasps sounded all around Kari. She froze, her limbs stiff and unmoving. Why in the world would that man give up one hundred thousand dollars to have dinner with her? It wasn't normal. He had to be a serial killer or something. Maybe even a deranged man looking to lock her up in his basement and turn her into his slave. Normal people did not give up that kind of money for a date. At least, none of the people she knew.

"One hundred thousand going once. Twice. Sold to number thirty for one hundred thousand dollars," the director said with a laugh. "Please meet Ms. Roma at the payment area. I have to tell you folks, these last two bids have been enough to help us keep our wild bear institute running for a few more years without worrying about funds. You are amazing!"

The crowd stood and clapped. Kari descended the stairs, and Julie stood there with a frown. "This is so weird. Both you and Penny have gotten the highest bids by men neither of you know. Something strange is going on here."

Yeah, like the possibility that Kari was about to go off to live in some psycho's basement. She swallowed at the lump in her throat and tried to smile at Julie who was the next one up for bid. "I have to go, but for all we know, you're going to end up getting a few million when you get up there."

Julie rolled her eyes. "Only if whoever buys me is insane."

"I'm starting to feel like whoever just bought me has to be crazy." She started walking away and waved at Julie. "Good luck!"

The man at the payment area wasn't familiar. "Hi, I'm Kari. You bid for some time with me?"

The guy grinned. "Hello, Kari. I'm Darren. Do you mind if our date is a bit off the beaten path?"

She shrugged. "You paid one hundred thousand dollars. If you feel like mud-wrestling with the hours we have left, I would accommodate you after giving up such a generous donation."

He was only an inch or two taller than her, which helped her feel a little better and less paranoid.

"Don't worry, nothing that crazy."

"You're not taking me to your home, are you?" The basement warning flashed in her mind.

"No, there's a restaurant a friend of mine owns not too far from here, and I had hoped you'd enjoy it. It's not in the city though. It's closer to the edge of the forest, and I thought you might like that."

She nodded and followed him out of the hotel to an awaiting limo. "Okay, but before we get in this car, I have to warn you, I have pepper spray and a Taser, and I know how to use both."

He chuckled and opened her door. "This should be fun."

After a short fifteen-minute ride, during which Darren made idle chit chat with her, he opened the door and helped her out of the car in front of what appeared to be a closed restaurant. She turned to face him with a frown. "It looks like they're closed for the night."

He laughed. "It is for everyone else. This is a great friend, and he's letting me use it to take a lovely lady out for the evening."

She wasn't sure if she should be happy or worried, but since her instinct wasn't screaming for her to get the hell out of there, she decided to give him the benefit of the doubt.

"Go on in. I'm just going to send the limo driver on his way," Darren said.

She strolled up the wooden steps and entered the restaurant. "Hello?"

The sound of tires on gravel told her the limo was gone. She turned around to the front door, waiting for Darren to enter, but he didn't.

"Kari."

She swirled on her heels and almost fainted when she saw Ash standing there, looking amazing in a tux and boldly gazing at her with an open hunger she'd come to know long ago.

"What are you doing here?" She walked backward toward the door. "I don't know what sick plan this is, but you and I broke up a year ago."

"No. You decided you couldn't cope with my schedule and left."

She stopped, her anger simmering in her veins. "You have got to be kidding me. I was the only one in the relationship."

He marched toward her, and she made a move to leave, but he reached her and flipped her around to face him. "No. Don't run now. You know I speak the truth."

"As you see it. How very fucking convenient." She tried to pull out of his hold, but he'd maneuvered around so she couldn't do anything with her back against the glass wall and his body pinning her.

"It's not how I see it. It's how it happened."

"Give me a fucking break," she snapped. "Why am I even here? When I broke up with you, I had to do it over the phone, because you weren't around, Ash. If that doesn't tell you how little you cared, then maybe this will: I will not be in a relationship by myself."

"You were never in a relationship by yourself. The company was taking off at a faster pace than I expected. I took on more than I could handle when I should have been delegating."

"I was an afterthought for you." She glanced away from his too-tempting face and wiggled, trying to escape his hold. "This isn't funny, Ash. You spent all that money on the auction. All you had to do was pay attention to me when you had me, and we wouldn't be here now."

"I didn't realize you felt forgotten," he said, curling his hand on her jaw, his warm fingers sending shivers down her spine.

THREE

Ash sensed the hurt Kari felt and wanted to kick his own ass. He'd done that to the one person he swore he wouldn't hurt.

"It doesn't matter now," she said, the waver in her voice jerking his bear into a frenzy.

"It does matter. For the past year I've been half-living without you."

She gave a bitter laugh. "Really? I'm sorry it's been so hard on you. But you can't really think I care when I spent countless nights alone after you'd promised you'd be back but weren't."

He hated that she was right. He'd allowed his job to consume him. It wasn't that he needed the money. It was that he wanted to prove he could do what he set out to do. She'd given him a lot more than he'd ever expected from a mate. But in his search for validation, he'd ignored the one person who mattered: her.

"It can be different now."

She glared at him, her eyes filled with anger. Finally, she pushed him. "Get the hell out of here.

You don't think I remember you saying that to me before? 'I'll be back in time for dinner' or 'of course, I'll be here for our date.' I've heard it all from you, Ash."

She shoved him, and he finally moved back, letting her loose. "Things are different. I'm different."

"Well I'm not. I'm still the same. And I still have the same expectations. I want a relationship between two people, not me and a cell phone," she growled.

"It won't be like that. I love you."

She rolled her eyes and stomped away. "Right."

His bear roared. She didn't believe him. That's the one thing he'd been open to her with—his feelings. He didn't do much of the romance, but he'd told her exactly how he felt. He stomped after her, stopping her by an empty table. "I was always truthful about my love for you, Kari."

"Really? Love? You call it love when I have to sit at home wondering when I'll see you again?"

"I told you—"

"I've gotten more love from my battery-operated toys, thank you very much. At least they stick around once I'm done."

His anger rose, and a rumble sounded in his chest. His bear pushed at the skin, wanting to shake some sense into his mate. He yanked her to him until he held her close. He slid one hand behind her back, grabbing a handful of her ass and pressing her pelvis close so she could feel his erection on her belly. He gripped her long hair, holding her face mere inches away. "You're playing with fire."

She licked her bottom lips and let out a short breath. "Why? I'm telling the truth. I got more love using my toys. Don't get angry when you know it's true."

"You can't compare a piece of plastic to me, not after the kind of response I got from your body." He rubbed his erection on her. Her sharp intake of breath was enough to let him know he got the point across. "Don't downgrade what we have always had."

"Had," she spit through clenched teeth. "Had. You fucked me. That's all there was to it."

"Oh no, baby." He squeezed her ass. He loved her body. She was so fucking hot with all her curves and that mouth that made him crazy. "What we had wasn't just fucking. I did fuck you, but there was more to it than that." He pressed his mouth to hers and quickly pulled back, unable to resist the tempting sight of her full, lush lips. "I owned your body. I didn't just take you. I stamped myself into your soul."

He watched arousal brighten to life in her eyes, growing with every breath she took.

"It was just sex."

He rocked his hips and watched her eyes glaze over with passion. "It was a lot more than sex, and you know it. You gave yourself to me fully. I don't give a fuck what you say now. We both know better."

She opened her mouth, and he saw the denial in her eyes. The bear pushed him, and he relented. He kissed her, hard. She struggled in his arms, and he loosened his hold only to have her grip his tux and shove the jacket open. He groaned. Kissing her felt so good. Her lips on his was better than anything he'd had in the past year. Memories didn't do any justice to how much he liked touching her. She curled her tongue over his and raked her nails down his shirt, tugging it from his pants.

When he first met Kari, he'd known at first sight she was the woman for him, not because of his bear's mating instinct, but because when she smiled, the world stopped. His heartbeats had slowed to a crawl, and nothing mattered but seeing her smiling again.

He turned her around and steered her to the table at her back, until she was sitting on it, her legs cradling his crotch. Fuck, he wanted to be inside her so bad. For the past year, his every fantasy revolved around having Kari in his arms, naked, showing her how much he loved her.

She moaned into the kiss, jerking back and meeting his gaze. He saw the same need he felt reflected in her eyes. "Ash, we've been done."

"Not even close," he said, fluttering his lips over the racing heartbeat at the base of her throat. Her deep breaths pushed at the straining material of her gown, pushing her breasts out over the neckline of her dress. He kissed his way down to her chest and yanked the bodice down, freeing her tits. Fuck, that's one of the things he loved about her. She was full-figured all over. Big tits, big ass, big hips. Sex with her had never been about worrying over her being too fragile or delicate. He could pound into her to his heart's delight, and she'd only ask for more.

FOUR

Kari gasped at Ash's first suck of her nipple. Lord, she'd missed his mouth. That tongue! He was amazingly good with it. He curled it around in circles and sometimes did a motorized rotation that sent moisture straight down her pussy.

She shoved his suit jacket off and tugged at the shirt. Buttons popped and flew all over the place. She had never been able to do that to a man before. It spoke of her desperation to touch his skin.

Smooth, hot flesh met her palms as she stroked him under the shirt. His muscles bunched and shifted, making her fingertips tingle. She'd been in love with his body from the first moment she saw him naked. He wasn't even huge when it came to muscles. He had a well-defined body: washboard abs that made her think of licking her way down his body and a cock worthy of a damn trophy.

He sucked on her nipple, flicking his tongue back and forth and dragging moan after moan out of her. He tore her dress off. A quick glance down and she saw his hands no longer human. The soft sound of his claws tearing at the sides managed to turn her on even more. He pushed the pieces of gown away and left her in nothing but a pair of silky, wet panties.

He stepped back, his gaze roaming down her body. "This," he said. "Is mine."

She had a hard time finding the voice to argue with him, not when he pushed her tits together and licked from one to the other. Not when he moved down her belly rolls and kissed them on his way to her pussy.

Spreading her shaky legs wider, she tugged at the ties at the side of her panties before he got a chance to tear them off too.

"I can't fucking wait to eat your pussy out." He tugged the panties off her, leaving her folds open for his view. "You love my tongue in you, sucking down your honey and making you come."

How could she deny the truth? Sex between them had to be one of the most amazing experiences of her life. He'd been the first man to give her an orgasm with his mouth and his cock. For most of her life, she thought she'd been too frigid to have them during sex. Her exes said she thought too much and didn't get into it. Ash knew every touch that enflamed her. He knew what to say, what to do, and when to do it.

As much as she wanted him licking her pussy and giving her an orgasm that would leave her begging for more, she missed him inside her. Clutching clumps of his short hair, she pulled him up to his feet and met his golden gaze with her own. "Fuck. Me."

If she was going to give in to temptation, then she'd take him inside her now, before common sense returned.

"I intended to fuck you with my tongue first." He winked. There was the flirt she'd fallen far. "I wanted you all nice and wet, ready to take my cock."

She shook her head, breaths burning their way in and out of her lungs. "No." She slid her hands down to his waist and messed with his fly. His pants flew south, and his fully erect cock filled her palm. "I want you to fuck me. Drive your cock deep inside and remind me how good we were together."

His features tightened with wild arousal. "I can do that, baby."

He hauled her closer to the table's edge and placed the head of his cock at her entrance. "I missed you so fucking much, Kari."

She didn't want words that would make her confused. She just wanted the touch. Skin to skin. His body taking, owning, possessing her. For now, that was enough.

He pushed forward with a groan, their eyes locked in a battle of wills. She refused to speak of her love, not when she'd felt so hurt and alone in the past, but she would accept the pleasure only he could give her.

She leaned back on the table, holding her body up with her elbows. He pushed her knees up until her feet pressed at the table's edge, her pussy spread wider for him. She gulped at how much heat there was in his eyes. That spark of ownership he'd always shown in his gaze when he glanced at her curves. He moved forward in a swift thrust. Her lungs ached from lack of oxygen. She choked out a moan and gripped the tablecloth under her palms.

"Ash," she gasped. "Yesss."

"Like that? Like me deep inside you?"

She nodded, her muscles tightening without her consent. "Do it, Ash. Fuck me like you used to."

He pulled back, almost fully out of her, and pressed forward again. "I missed your body, baby. I missed every dip," he said, grabbing one of her breasts with his hand and thumbing her nipple. "Every curve. I missed how you scream when you come. It's so fucking hot. I missed the feel of your pussy sucking my dick when you were on top."

Lord, she'd missed that too. She'd missed him so damn much. She whimpered at the back of her throat as he moved faster. Harder. Deeper. Her body clamored for more of his thrusts. Every slide of him into her only made her want more. It was an addiction, a hunger she'd pushed to sleep. Now awake, she couldn't get enough. More. She needed more of him. All of him.

He pushed in and out. Over and over. Faster and harder. Her breasts bounced up and down. Her belly quivered with every drive.

"This is how I've been dreaming of you," he grunted, his abs contracting with every thrust. "Wide open. Wanting me in you. Begging for more of my cock." He licked his lips. "Do it. Beg me to fuck you, Kari."

"Please, Ash," she whimpered with no hesitation. "Fuck me more. Don't stop."

"I never planned on stopping," he breathed the words out in short bursts. "I won't stop. Not until I take you back as mine." His voice turned into a low growl. "Not until I've come inside you. Over you. Until my scent is everywhere on you."

Passion curled into a tight knot at her core. She could taste the oncoming orgasm. "Oh, my, god."

"Ah, baby. That's deep," he groaned, his hips rocking in a motion that pushed her body up on the table, but he yanked her back down with his hands. "Your pussy's deep and tight. So fucking wet and hot. I can't hold it much longer. I want to fill you with my cum."

Ash slid his hand down, rubbing her exposed clit with his thumb, and she choked out a long scream, her body unravelling. She lost control of her limbs. Everything shook as waves of bliss bathed her body with joy. Her pussy contracted hard around his cock. He stopped suddenly, his hands on her hips and his nails digging painfully at her sides.

"Fuck!" he roared as he came, filling her in long spurts with his seed.

She gasped, her legs shaking as she tried to sit up. He helped her up and stumbled back, falling into a chair and setting her down on his lap. She sat there for quiet moments, trying to catch her breath.

Once her common sense returned, she pushed away the feelings of guilt. She wasn't seeing anyone else, and she knew Ash well enough to know he wasn't either or he wouldn't have gotten her naked. Not that it had taken much to get her naked, but whatever.

She slipped off his lap and stared at what used to be her dress with a frown. What the hell was she supposed to wear now? His suit jacket was strewn next to her gown. She picked it up and put it on without saying a word. It would be easier to tell him this wasn't going to happen again with clothes on.

"So what prompted this?" she asked, turning to face him and catching him zipping up his pants. He made no attempt to put on the shirt. Bastard.

FIVE

Is brows rose, and a grin floated over his lips. "What? Me finally kicking my own ass and coming for the one woman I've ever loved?"

She didn't want to let it, but his words warmed her. She'd never truly believed he loved her. Not because he didn't say the words, but he just wasn't there to prove it. She'd lived most of their relationship alone.

"Yeah." She cleared her throat. "Something like that. Why now? Why did you wait almost a full year to do something about us?"

He shoved his hands in his pocket and leaned back by the restaurant's bar. "Stupidity. I wanted you to come back to me. I knew you loved me. I didn't think you were serious at first. That you really wanted to leave when we both knew we were right for each other. So good together."

She pursed her lips and folded her arms over her chest. "You really thought that sex would bring me back?" She shook her head. "You must not really know me then."

"It's not that I don't know you. I was so busy, Kari. Too busy. I thought you understood the responsibility I had in my hands. It was too much for one person to handle on his own." He scrubbed a hand over his jaw. "I realized after you left that I needed to take on less work and have a life."

Lovely. He'd realized, once she'd gotten tired of sitting around alone, to make time for a woman. She didn't want to ask him how many he'd been with in the past year. She'd later found out he was a bear-shifter and researched as much as possible about his species. It didn't surprise her to know he could turn into a giant bear. She'd known shifters existed and he had that big body that most normal men didn't have. Besides, she knew shifters loved them some curves. It surprised her to know how committed they could be when they found their mates.

"Why didn't you tell me you were a bear-shifter?" she asked.

He glanced down at the floor before meeting her gaze. "I…I didn't want to scare you."

She huffed a breath and stomped her foot. "Scare me? What the hell do I look like some weak little human? Why would you telling me you were a bear scare me?"

He grinned. "A lot of women get scared of shifters. They think we're going to hurt them somehow, during sex or if we become angry."

"Those women are clearly idiots." She rolled her eyes and turned away. "This is the kind of stuff we should have talked about but never could, because you weren't there. How is it that you're now ready but still holding things back? Until I asked you, I didn't see you being forthcoming with the information. Did you think I didn't realize how hard it was for you to stay human?"

He clenched his jaw and stared her down. "I would have told you. I wanted us to spend some time together again. I wanted to remind you how much you mean to me."

"Right now, all I'm seeing is that you are talking a lot and doing a poor job of convincing me of anything." She tossed her hair over her shoulder and glanced at the front door. "Do me a favor and take me home. Talking to you is clearly not going to get my point across."

He watched her for a long moment, his lips pressed into a thin line. "Fine."

She followed him out the door to the side of the restaurant where a bike was parked. "You're kidding right?" She glanced down at herself, then back at him. "I'm half-naked, Ash!"

He grinned. "Sorry, babe. It's either this or waiting awhile until the limo can come back and get us. I promise to take the empty back roads to get you home."

She debated for all of thirty seconds and got on the bike. The motor purred to life and vibrated between her legs. She curled her arms around his waist and snuggled tight to his back. She was glad his jacket was long and covered her back, but there was no way to cover the large amount of thigh she showed off. She'd just have to deal with it.

He handed her a helmet and took off. True to his word, he took empty back roads and quiet side streets until they reached her house. She slipped off the bike and motioned for him to stay on it. "I'm fine. I can get myself inside."

He nodded, his features passive. She couldn't really tell what he was thinking, but this wasn't the end of things. That much she knew about Ash. Once he'd decided she'd be his, he had been persistent. Not that she had given him much of a fight. She'd been too attracted to him herself.

"Good night, Ash."

"Think about what you want. Because you'll have to make a choice soon. Really soon."

He left her standing there, thinking back to the words he'd said. What did she want? She'd never wanted anyone but Ash since she'd met him. Even when she'd given up on their relationship, she'd secretly hoped he'd come for her, at least at the beginning. After a while she knew his job had been more important than anything they had.

SIX

The following morning, she'd just gotten dressed to go run some errands when her doorbell rang. She opened the door to Ash, wearing a pair of jeans that hugged his large legs like a dream. A black T-shirt clung to his torso and showed off the abs she'd fallen in lust with.

"Wow. Wasn't expecting to see you here."

"Good morning." He grinned, handing her a to-go cup she had a suspicion contained her favorite coffee.

A quick sip confirmed her thoughts. He was bribing her with her favorite drink, and she didn't really care why. It was early. She was grumpy without coffee.

"Good morning," she grumbled.

"I hope you're not too busy today. I have a surprise for you." He smiled wide. Her heart flipped in her chest, and pleasure heated her blood. In the past, Saturdays had meant him being at work, so for him to be there and not at his office was a pretty big deal in her book.

"Depends. Is there more coffee involved in this outing?"

She'd spent the previous night thinking about what she wanted in her life. She still loved Ash, no doubt about that. Why deny the truth? What she wasn't going to put up with was taking a backseat to his job again. She knew that for sure. If he was sincere in putting her above the crazy amount of work and travel he'd done in the past, then she couldn't see why she shouldn't give him a chance. Truth was, she didn't want to push him away when she knew he was the only man she loved. He'd never done anything to hurt her so badly that a second chance couldn't be warranted.

He laughed and motioned to his sports car with his head. That was another thing. He was rich. Like fucking loaded. She hadn't realized how well off he'd been in the past, because he worked like his bank account depended on it. So when she found out from a news article that her man was one of the town's most eligible bachelors with enough money to buy the whole damn state, she'd been more than a little pissed he hadn't told her.

"I will get you all the coffee you want," he promised, his blue eyes dancing with laughter. "Come on, we have to get going to do what we have to do."

She might regret it later, but she'd try. Ash was the love of her life. It'd be stupid of her to ignore her feelings.

* * *

Ash watched Kari's face pale.

"Sky diving? Are you out of your ever-loving mind?" She gasped. "The last time we did this, I was drunk and strapped to you. Why would I want to do this again?"

He laughed. "Because this time you won't be drunk. Therefore, no getting sick when we land. And you will still be strapped to me, darling."

She narrowed her eyes, slapping her hands on her hips. Gorgeous hips that urged him to get her naked whenever he glanced at them. "I will have you know, I am not in the mood to try that shit again. So think again, Romeo."

He shook his head and lifted her hand to his lips. "I see you've gone back to your term of endearment for me. I like that. But why don't you just do it this one time, and I promise it will be worth it."

She nibbled on her lip and glanced at the plane. "I don't know…"

"Come on. If you never want to do it again after this, I will never ask. I promise."

She sighed, a look of defeat covering her features. "Fine, but if I get sick, I am not talking to you again."

"Ouch!" He pressed her hand to his chest. "I said it will be worth it, and I mean it."

They wore some special helmets that covered the back of their heads and ears, with microphones attached so he could talk to her on their way down. There was a small screen at the top of hers that showed her his face and vice versa. This way he could see her reaction to the drop on their way down. Last time he hadn't thought to do it, but this time he needed to see her face. Twenty minutes later, they stood at the edge of the plane, wind howling in their ears and nearly pushing them off their feet.

"Ready?" he said into his mic.

"Yes, you crazy man. I can't believe you talked me into this again!" she yelled with a smile, her gaze on the clouds below them.

He counted to three, and they jumped. Her scream and wide-eyed wonderment made it that much more amazing for him. He'd skydived hundreds of times but never had it been this special.

"Kari," he screamed into his mic, knowing that the speed and wind would make it almost impossible for her to hear.

"Yes?"

He tugged on the parachute strap, and things slowed down. "I love you."

She laughed and glanced at the tiny camera shooting her face. "I love you, too."

They were getting closer to the ground. Showtime.

"Look over to your left side. The field by the big water tower," he said.

"Is that…? Oh my god!"

He laughed at her scream just as they were nearing ground. He maneuvered the parachute until their feet touched the ground and dragged them forward about five feet before coming to a complete stop. He untangled them from the chute, unbuckling both and letting them separate.

She flipped around to face him, taking the helmet off and staring at him with wide eyes.

"Is that…? Is that for real?"

He nodded, looking at the rows of hay that formed the words 'Marry Me?' "I was stupid in the past, letting you go and not even bothering to admit my mistakes."

He got down on one knee, watching her eyes widen even more and her lip tremble. "Will you marry me, Kari? Make me the happiest bear in this city?"

She nodded, her eyes filling with moisture. "Yes. I will."

He jumped to his feet and hugged her tight, kissing her for all he was worth. He'd made mistakes and could understand that things with them hadn't lasted as long as he'd hoped their last round, but now was a chance for him to make sure they both got the love that they deserved.

SEVEN

Kari held on to Ash as he carried her through her door. "You know, I can walk."

He laughed. "I know. I love holding you. Besides, you weigh next to nothing."

She snorted. "Yeah, right. Tell that to my doctor. According to him, I need to be working out 24/7 to get the body he thinks I need."

He frowned and continued on to her bedroom. "Screw the doctor. You should get a new one if he's being that much of an asshole. You're not a junk-food eater, and you work out."

They'd spent the entire day together today. After he'd given her the ultimate proposal while skydiving, he took her to a local fair, and they got on a bunch of rides. It was like being a teenager all over again. Only this time, she was the girl with the hot boyfriend, not the one everyone swore needed an attitude adjustment.

His cell phone went off just as he put her on the bed. She frowned, watching him reach for it.

His shoulders dropped, and he answered. "Hey, what's going on?"

She started undressing, ready to take a bath, and overheard him talk.

"Now? This can't wait for another time?" He cursed. "Look, I don't see how I can do that now. I'm not in the office. I'd need to get over there and put it together."

Her heart sank. It was a Saturday, and already his job was trying to take him away. She didn't bother saying anything, just marched into the bathroom, closing the door softly at her back.

This was what she worried about. His intense focus on the job meant she'd lose precious time with him. It wasn't that she disliked the fact that he worked. Heck, she did too. But what annoyed her was how he didn't seem to realize that his overworking put her in a position of feeling unwanted. Unneeded. Like he was too busy, and she was in his way.

She turned on the spray of water and pushed away the anxiety curling up her spine, robbing her of the previous happiness she'd been floating on.

"Stupid," she mumbled, standing under the spray of warm water and sighing. She should have known it was too good to be true, that his job might continue coming between them.

"I refuse to let you call yourself names," he said, grabbing her arm and turning her to face him.

She squinted under the water, staring at his sinful grin. "What happened? I thought for sure you'd have to leave?"

It was at that moment she realized that she she'd been expecting the worst from him, for him to do the same thing he had in the past. Guilt crept over her. How could she have done that? He'd been nothing but honest in what he'd said, in acknowledging his guilt.

He held her face with his hands. "You have so little faith in me. You think after I told you what I did that I could then go and do the opposite."

She swallowed at the lump in her throat. "I'm sorry. I did think the worst. It was my usual reaction when it comes to you and your job."

He pushed her back, until her back hit the tiled wall and his wet body pressed on her front. "I wouldn't do that to you. It might have taken me a while, but I did realize you leaving was the worst thing to happen to me."

"Why?"

"Without you, I lose my drive. I lose my reason for wanting to be a better person. I worked so hard to make myself proud, but at the same time show you I could be more than a rich guy."

She lifted her hands up to his waist, pulling him to her and gasping at the hardness of his erection. "I didn't realize how much of a rich guy you were. I thought you must have been struggling to be so keen on working any hour to build up the business."

"No. I wanted you to be proud of me. I see how hard you work at making the non-profit flourish. Between you, Penny, and Julie, you have made the company grow with just donations you secured. I wanted to have something like that in my life. Something I could feel good about."

She lifted up to her toes and brushed her lips over his. "I'm proud of you, Ash. You've done amazing things with the company, along with your brothers. You've done it all while the world talks about you guys like you're only sexy men with no brains. I know it sucks to read more articles about what you wear than what you're doing with the company. That's the media for you. I know better. I see your internal struggle and your success."

His lips came crashing down over hers. A world of need opened up under her feet. She clung to him, letting her body dictate what came next. He pushed his tongue into her mouth, his aggression welcome in the heat of the moment. Gasps rushed up her throat. Water rained down over them, cooling some of the sizzle rising from her limbs.

His arm muscles bunched as he cupped both her breasts and fondled her tits. His cock pressed at her belly, searching for her slick entrance and ready to take her to new heights of passion. She'd always loved that about Ash. He wanted her, wanted her body.

His absolute desire for her big curves and wide hips sent her heart soaring. She'd known she looked great, but some men acted like she should bow down to them because she was the fat chick and needed the attention. Fuck that. Ash was a good looking sweet man who genuinely loved her body. He loved her as she was. She'd loved him the same.

He tore his lips from her. His gaze kept her rooted to the cool wall. "Let me love you, Kari."

Oh, yes. She wanted him to love her. To take her. Hell, she'd let him do any and everything to her as long as he continued.

"I thought you already did," she moaned, her nails scoring long red lines on his arms.

She didn't get a chance to catch her breath before he had her flipped, her hands on the metal rod she'd had installed for her washcloths. He bit his fingers into her hips, tugging her back until his cock pressed between her cheeks. "I do love you, beautiful. But now I want to fuck your wet pussy." He caressed a hand down her spine, shooting electricity up to her neck. "I want to feel your cunt clasping my cock with every drive. Oh, I want you moaning. Groaning. Screaming my fucking name."

She gasped, her body winding as he pressed into her, his shaft filling her channel with his hardness. She moaned more the further he went. It was so sexy. Then, to add to her already-aroused state, he threaded his fingers through chunks of her hair and tugged, making her look over her shoulder at him. He propelled back and sank deep.

"Yes, Kari. That's what I like to see. The glaze of pleasure in your eyes." He reeled his hips back and thrust again.

She gasped, her eyes closing out of their own free will. "Ash…"

"Do it, baby. Say my name like that again. Like I'm a fucking god." He moved faster. Harder. Slapping his hips into her ass.

She gripped the bar hard, almost expecting it to break, but it didn't. Instead, her knuckles burned from how tight she held on. Ash licked the back of her shoulder and stopped for a nibble by her ear. "I can't tell you how hot it is to watch my dick going in and out of your pussy."

She bit her lip, water still raining over them in a warm spray. "God, Ash. I feel you deep. So deep."

"You...," he grunted, his drives jerking her up and closer to the cliff she'd been looking for since the last time they were together, "...say the sexiest things, love."

She didn't know about that. He did feel fucking huge inside her. And hot. She wanted to come, but at the same time didn't want to stop feeling him taking her. "Shit! Ash, I'm so close."

"Then let's take you closer," he rumbled by her ear. "Let's watch that beautiful face of yours as you come." He nibbled on her lobe. "Personally, that's better than any porn I've ever watched. Your face in bliss makes me harder than a fucking rock."

He yanked her hair back, and she whimpered. The bite of pain in her scalp wasn't one she was used to, but for some reason it didn't bother her. It enhanced all of it.

Releasing the bar, she slapped a hand on her chest, tweaking a nipple before sliding it down the curve of her belly, between her legs. She pressed on her clit, gasping and groaning at how good it felt. He pumped harder and curled a hand around her hip, pressing it over hers.

Though her moves on her clit had been light and barely grazing the super-sensitive bit of flesh, his fingers plucked and pressed on it with a lot more force. Molten lava heated at her core. She tensed, her muscles all but losing their ability to keep her upright.

"Ash, oh, Ash!" she screeched, her orgasm shot through her hard, taking her by surprise.

It wasn't a slow, sweet coming like she'd had in the past. This time it felt as if a ball had broken inside her and sent pleasure skidding through her veins, stinging her from the inside, stopping her very ability to breathe.

He let go of her hair, and she dropped her head forward, watching his fingers turn to claws at her hips. They bit down on her flesh, drawing blood where every tip had embedded in her skin. She couldn't care less. It hurt, but his cock fucking her like he never had was worth it. She choked out breaths, her pussy still grasping at his cock with the contractions from a new set of mini-orgasms ripping through her.

He roared by her ear, his claws yanked back, leaving a burning sensation on both hips as he came inside her. Spots danced before her eyes. She could barely stand, but none of that mattered. He continued filling her with his warm essence. Something about him taking her and losing control to the point that his fingers had shifted made it even more erotic. He'd scratched her hard.

He pulled out of her, hugging her back to his chest and holding her under the spray of water.

"You're mine now, beautiful."

She grinned and rested her head on his shoulder. "I thought I already was. Isn't that what your proposal was all about?"

He laughed. "Yes. But now the bear wanted to claim you. The scars on your hips aren't going anywhere. They'll stay there forever, proof that you belong to us."

She wasn't fond of the "belonging" word, but she knew he meant it in the best possible way. So she'd accept being his, as long as he was hers.

EIGHT

"Wake up, babe." Ash tugged on her blanket. "You must be suicidal. Why would you wake me up at the crack of dawn?"

He laughed. "It's only four. Come on, I have a surprise for you."

She groaned. "The last time you had a surprise for me I got to jump out of a plane."

She didn't really mind the memory, though. He'd proposed to her. That was a lot more special than she'd ever expected from any man. She didn't break up with Ash because she wanted to get married. She broke up with him because it didn't appear their relationship existed in his life. At all. Now, he made a lot more time than he ever had. For the past week, he'd worked from home and made sure to stop once she stopped to spend time with her.

"Come, I'll have breakfast and coffee, and you're going to love it."

She grumbled her way out of bed and took a shower. Forty-five minutes later, they were on a helicopter, being lifted into the dark sky. "At least this time I'm not expected to jump, right? Or you would have provided a parachute?"

He winked, his blue eyes bright with excitement. "Trust me here."

She grinned. "I do. That's the crazy part. I have to be just as insane as you to be doing whatever it is we're doing without questioning it."

He twined his fingers with hers. "You trust me. I'll never break your trust."

She did trust him. Fully. In the past, men had come and gone, though not many. But she learned that when it came to love, she needed someone who would accept her as she came. Bitchiness and all. Ash had done that. He'd never tried to curb her snark, or anything else about her personality. What he had done was laugh at some of the things she said.

The helicopter started to descend on a patch of land on top of a mountain she'd never been to. She could see trees surrounding the entire area, and then they were jumping out and moving out of the way. A few moments later it was quiet all around them.

She hadn't noticed any light, but upon glancing around she saw some lanterns between the trees.

"Come on. You'll like this, I promise."

She sighed. "I didn't have to climb the tree or hike, so I'm already liking it."

He pulled her by the hand, toward the lights. Small, paper lanterns had been set up to light up a walkway between the trees. It wasn't a long walk before she saw the opening between the trees. They came out into a large clearing by the edge of one of the mountain's cliffs. A giant blanket with a picnic had been set up. She glanced up to meet his gaze.

"I told you you'd like it."

She eyed the covered plates and grinned. "Like it? I love it!"

She threw herself in his arms, giving him a tight hug and only pulling back to kiss him. She ran her fingers through his hair and lowered her head to his shoulder. This was what she'd hoped for their last time together.

"Come on, sweetheart. I've got food, and you're going to love it," he said helping her down on the blanket.

She noticed the big, portable coffee container and sighed. He was right. She was going to love it all right.

He served their coffees, and she folded her legs to get more comfortable. They didn't bother with the food just yet. He took his paper cup and sat beside her, hugging her to his side and glancing out at the dark city below them.

"I can't tell you how sorry I am for not realizing what a dickhead I was being in the past."

She stared out at the horizon, the orange and gold colors of the dawn lightening up the darkness out in the distance and allowing her to see everything around them. "This is such an amazing view."

He kissed the side of her head. "I know. I couldn't think of a better way for us to restart our relationship than to watch the dawning of a new day."

She gulped at the emotions clogging her throat. "We all make mistakes."

He sighed. "I know, but mine almost cost me losing you forever."

She shook her head. "I don't know. This time apart has taught you how to work and have a life. Maybe that's what you needed."

"I won't let my job come between us again," he promised, his big hand caressing up and down her arm.

"Hey, if you do, I know that you just need a kick in the ass next time."

He barked a laugh and lifted his coffee cup. "To us."

She shook her head. "To not being forgotten."

"Baby, I could never forget you. You're the one person in my life I can't live without."

She grinned at him. "Sometimes we lose sight of what's important, but as long as your ass doesn't forget your promises to me, we're okay."

"I can only hope Julie and Penny are this forgiving with Ethan and Rafe."

She gasped. "You guys did that, didn't you? Set up the whole buying us for tons of money just to get time with us."

"You're the only person I'd give up my entire fortune for."

Happiness pulled a smile wide over her lips. "I love you!"

"I love you too, beautiful." He inhaled deep and let it out slow. "Think the others will take a hint from you and make my brothers' lives easier?"

Kari pursed her lips in a pout. "I don't work miracles. Those guys are in for a hell of a time."

Poor bastards. She wondered how Julie fared with Rafe. Penny called out of work due to being sick, but Julie had taken off, and they hadn't seen or heard from her for the past week. She could only assume she and Rafe were working on their problems.

Kari grinned. "I love you, Ash. You're lucky I'm the nicest of the three of us."

He chuckled, cupping her jaw and lifting her face so he could look into her eyes. "I'm lucky for a lot of reasons. That one might be the biggest one," he said, lowering his head to kiss her.

FUR-GIVEN

ONE

Julie Durante glanced at her computer screen. So maybe she had a small obsession with her ex. Nobody needed to know. Rafe Sinclair had given her the most amazing months of her life. He'd also dumped her when she refused to commit. The news article she was reading showed a photo of Rafe and his two brothers going into a restaurant.

Her eyes ate up the vision of Rafe with his usual frown and super-serious features. Her friends didn't know that he'd dumped Julie. They thought the opposite had taken place. The thing was that mating didn't translate to love in Rafe's book. For Julie, love didn't equal mating. So she was more than happy refusing to mate until Rafe admitted his feelings for her. How could a man be so pig-headed?

She should be getting dressed for the ball, not sighing and wondering what the hell Rafe was up to. Most days she was good and kept her obsession with him in check. Then there were those times some society column had the three eligible bears on the front cover of the paper.

"What are you looking at?" Lizzie, her sister and roommate, asked.

"Nothing," she replied, slamming the laptop closed with a bang.

"Too late. I saw your man in the photo. Why don't you just go see him?" Lizzie asked. "It's not like you can't."

Julie hopped to her feet and faced her sister. "He dared to break up with me when he was the one who couldn't open up."

"Um, he told you that if you didn't commit he would. You didn't commit. What did you think would happen?"

Julie growled. "I know I didn't commit. I wasn't going to sign up for a lifetime of him telling me he wanted me but refusing to admit his love."

"Oh, please. You knew he loved you."

She did. She had realized it from the first. His knowing was another story. He'd given her long hours of telling her how much he desired her, how much he loved her body, how he didn't want any woman but her. Want. Great word. Not as good as love, though. That was the problem.

So when Rafe had told her he wanted her as his mate, to be in a long-term relationship with him and bear his children, she almost fainted from joy. Almost. Until she realized he had yet to admit to himself that he loved her. So she'd said no. She wasn't going to give him the easy way out and allow him to use want as a replacement for love. She hadn't counted on him being as hardheaded as her. He'd pushed her until she openly rejected him. Then came the breakup.

"I knew he loved me, yes. He didn't seem to have any fucking clue."

She marched to her bedroom and threw a closet door open, the wood banging against the wall. Now she had this stupid auction to deal with. Where the hell were her new gowns?

"Are you blind, Jules?" Lizzie asked, pointing at the rack next to the bed. Four ball gowns hung from it in clear plastic coverings. "You put the dresses out here."

She glared at Lizzie and frowned at the options. Why did she let herself get caught up in the moment when it came to shopping? Whether it was shoes, handbags, or dresses, she could spend all her money buying more than she could wear.

"So pick one for me." She pursed her lips. "The gold one is nice. Makes my skin look nice and healthy."

"You need sex appeal…," Lizzie said. "… that stuff you have in more doses than the regular woman."

Julie grinned. "I do not."

"Do so. You have got to be one of the few curvy women I know that will strut her stuff without giving a shit." Lizzie smiled wide. "You're my hero, big sis."

Well, she did do that. She wasn't ashamed of her body, and whoever was needed to look the fuck away. She was big. Curvy. Plumpy. Whatever the hell people wanted to call it, she was fine with it. She knew she'd never get another body, so why dislike the one she had? A woman was supposed to have curves. Julie just had more than the average woman. She was really big and really bold. And she was perfectly happy with that.

"Never mind that. Help me pick a dress. I'm going to be late, and it's all stupid Rafe's fault. Even though I haven't been in the same room with him in almost a year, I can't get the bastard out of my mind."

Lizzie snorted a giggle. "I don't think you can blame your brain for that. He is one hot-as-hell man. Have you seen the face on him and his brothers?"

"Liz?"

"Yeah, okay. You've seen it. Every one of them is like every woman's dream man come true. They're huge but not uber muscular, with that mountain-man size and a rough and rugged face. I tell ya, I felt my ovaries drop when I first met the three of them."

Julie burst into laughter. She couldn't blame Lizzie. Julie's hormones had gone all kinds of wild the first time she'd met Rafe Sinclair. He'd pulled her to the side at an event for her job and proceeded to tell her all the really dirty things that came to mind when he looked at her. How in the world could a woman in her right mind refuse a hot-as-sin man like him? To make matters worse, he didn't just talk a good game. Rafe had a mouth on him worthy of every dollar in her savings. She missed him in every sense of the word. Daily.

Coming from an upper-middle class family, she'd never really given money much thought. When she found out that Rafe and his brothers were loaded, it hadn't really made much of a difference to her. She worked for her money, and she had a healthy savings. What he had wasn't her business. She knew that he worked damn hard, so they both deserved every penny they had.

"Come on, Jules. Pick a dress that you feel good in, and let's get to work on that hair of yours. We don't have all night," Lizzie grumbled, assembling brushes, combs, and a curling iron on Julie's vanity.

"I'm going, I'm going. Fine. The silver. I think I have great sandals that go with it," she said, rushing toward the bathroom.

"As long as you don't break your neck on that stage, we'll be fine."

TWO

Rafe Sinclair paced his house. He didn't like the idea of bringing Julie to him under false pretenses. He stopped by the window overlooking the city to the left and the forest to the right. It was the only way he could manage to stay sane in an enclosed place, not that he spent much of his time in the penthouse. In fact, he hardly ever stayed there since he and Julie broke up.

"What's going on?" Ethan asked, coming up behind him. "I can tell you're pissed."

"I don't like the idea of deceiving Julie."

Ethan shook his head. "It's not really deception. It's just trying to find a way to spend some time and talk to her. You may not have realized it, but being without her has turned you into a miserable old man, bro."

Rafe raised a brow and walked to the bar. "You called me that before I met her."

Ethan grinned. "Yeah, but now you've really made it your mission in life to be in a sour disposition all the time."

He filled a glass with whiskey and brought it to his lips. "Really?"

"Let me put it to you this way, old man: Kyle and Ash have bets on how many times you'll smile in a day."

"Get the fuck out of here!" he snapped. "What the hell does me smiling have anything to do with Julie?"

"Kyle's winning," Ethan said, ignoring his question. "He says you'll never smile again until you're back with her."

Fucking hell. Maybe the annoying kid had something. Since things had gone to hell between him and Julie, Rafe hadn't been able to enjoy anything anymore. Not running through the forest. Not hunting. And certainly not sex. There had been no fucking of any kind since Julie. That made the bear angry. The fact that Rafe had pushed her away added to his misery. He knew she'd been right in asking for him to open up about his emotions and tell her how he felt, but he didn't see the importance. She knew he loved her. So what the hell was the big deal?

Still, he didn't want to continue living in misery. Without his mate, that's where he was. In a miserable hellhole that never went away.

"Don't you want to talk to her? To get a chance to set things straight?" Ethan put on the bow tie that went with his tux. "She hasn't dated anyone else since you."

"How do you know?"

Ethan gave him a look. "The same way I know Penny hasn't been on a date since we broke up— Kyle. We all have him keeping track of our women but refuse to make the effort to bridge the gap between us. It ends today."

Rafe hated to admit it, but his brother was right. He needed to hash things out with Julie. But he couldn't see waiting until some guy delivered her to him. Fuck that. He wanted to go out and get his woman himself.

"I'm going to that auction."

Ethan slapped a hand on his shoulder. "What are you thinking? That's not part of the plan."

"I don't care," Rafe said. He turned to face Ethan and shook his head. "I want her to know I'm the one paying for her time."

"That could bring all sorts of problems, Rafe. What if she refuses to leave with you?"

He shrugged. "I'll figure it out. It's not like I'm going to walk out of that place without her. I'll have a talk with Theo and make sure he helps out."

Ethan sighed. "If that's what you want to do, I understand. I wish I was there to see Penny, but I think she might throw something at me and create a scene."

Rafe smiled. "I'm hoping Julie creates a scene. It'll make it easier for me to get her out of there without having to debate with her."

"You're crazy, bro." Ethan laughed. "I've gotta go, and so do you if you're going to make it in time."

"I will. I'm just going to let you know right now that I'm going to take some days off and figure things out with Julie."

Ethan nodded. "I understand. I'm going to do the same with Penny. She has to see nothing's more important than she is."

Rafe had to do more than just show Julie she was important to him. If what the guys thought was true, then he needed to remind himself how to enjoy his life, ideally with her by his side.

THREE

Julie frowned. Something weird was going on. Penny had been bought for fifty thousand dollars. That was a huge amount of money. Then, it got even weirder when Kari was bought for one hundred thousand. That right there was insane. Insane.

Kari walked away from Julie, heading to the payment area.

"Our next lady up for bid is Ms. Julie Durante."

Fuck. She glanced around the floor, looking for anyone that might seem out of place, but she was distracted by a hand poking at her back.

"Julie? It's your turn, dear," Meredith, Dave's wife, said. "I'm so excited!" she gushed. "I cannot wait to see what your winning bid will be. Think it could go as high as Karina's?"

"No way in hell!" she replied and turned her back on Meredith. She went up to the stage, stood behind the curtains, and hesitated.

"Ms. Durante?" The director said into the mic. "Don't be shy. We're all here for charity."

She ground her teeth and pasted a fake smile on her face, sashaying to the center of the stage.

"There she is. My, isn't she a lovely one?" the director said.

She almost rolled her eyes. Screw lovely. She was fucking gorgeous, but she might be a bit biased.

"Ms. Durante has a shoe fetish she feeds on a regular basis."

She frowned. What the hell? She glared over her shoulder at the director, but he continued reading as if nothing was wrong.

"She loves to boss people around, and she likes playing old-school video games. Now, let's open up the bids for Ms. Durante."

She glanced at the crowd. Charlie waved from the bar, nodding and letting her know he was there. Her smile widened.

The director cleared his throat. "Do I hear one thousand dollars?"

Damn! The man had started out high. What happened to warming the crowd up with a few hundred?

Charlie raised his number. "One thousand dollars."

Good man, Charlie. She'd given permission to bid up to ten thousand dollars, just because it was for charity…that and she didn't want to be sold for a hundred bucks. Now that she saw a hundred was never even considered, she was glad she'd given up more.

"Do I hear two thousand?" the director asked.

She blinked. What the hell? Why was he going up so high?

"Two thousand dollars," said an old guy sitting off in one of the last tables at the back.

Aw, hell. Trust her to end up with one of the lecherous old men.

"Thee thousand," Charlie yelled.

"Five thousand," the old man countered.

Her breaths started coming in short bursts, and her palms slickened with sweat.

"Ten thousand," Charlie said, giving up her full donation.

"I haven ten thousand dollars. Do I hear eleven?" the director said. Silence reigned in the room for a heartbeat. "Ten thousand going once. Ten thousand going twice."

"One million dollars," said a loud, firm voice she knew all too well.

Her eyes scanned the room, until she found him: Rafe. A hum of whispers sounded in the crowd.

"No," she said.

"Excuse me?" The director asked.

She turned to face him. "You can't take his bid. He can't possibly have one million dollars."

The director raised his brows and glanced at Rafe. "Mr. Sinclair, do you have a check at hand?"

The man standing next to Rafe waved the check. "Mr. Sinclair is ready to pay."

"Well, I guess that solves that." The director smiled. Panic threaded through Julie's limbs. "One million dollars going once. Twice. Sold to Mr. Rafe Sinclair for one million dollars."

She narrowed her eyes, her anger fully directed at the bear. How dare he do that to her?

She stomped away from the stage, rushing down the steps.

"Ladies and gentlemen," the director said, "our most successful bachelorette auction is now over. Thank you for your donations. Please enjoy the rest of your evening with the music and food we've arranged for you."

She wove her way through the crowd of people standing to dance. The band started playing, and the joy of having raised almost 1.2 million dollars for the company had everyone giddy…except for her.

Rafe stood in the center of the room, surrounded by Dave, his wife, and the director. She didn't bother stopping; instead she headed straight for the door.

Once outside, she motioned for a cab but none stopped.

"I didn't take you for a runner," Rafe said behind her.

She turned on her heels. "Really? Me? The runner? I don't think so. I'm the one that actually gave a shit."

FOUR

He came closer, his size towering over her even though she had on some of her highest heels. "I gave a shit, Julie. I gave you a lot more than I ever gave anyone."

"It wasn't enough. You held back. You broke my heart, and now you're here, acting like some rich asshole who can just buy his way into my life." She slapped her hands on her hips. "Have you forgotten that I have my own fucking money. Did you think I'd be impressed with you trying to buy me for the night?"

He marched closer, until she was but a foot away from him. "I am not trying to buy you. I only want some time to talk."

She stomped her foot on the ground. "So talk to yourself."

"I came here for you," he bit out.

"And I'm leaving because of you." She turned away, ready to try her hand at the oncoming taxis. He grabbed her arm and stopped her.

"You're not going anywhere until we talk."

"Fuck you, Rafe," she snapped, tugging on her arm. "You think you can just come here, and I have to listen? No. I don't. It's called free-fucking-will, and you don't own me."

"I already know that," he growled, hauling her into his arms. "Fucking hell, Julie. Just listen."

"No." She struggled, trying to break free, but he didn't budge.

"Fine. You want it the hard way, huh? I can do that for you, princess," he said and lifted her in his arms, tossing her on his shoulder.

She screamed. Rafe was the first and only man to ever be able to lift her without losing his breath. It was scary and exciting. He held her with one arm and slammed a hand over her ass. "Stay still, or I swear I'll tear that fucking dress off you right here and give these people a real show."

She lifted her head, trying to see past the curls in front of her eyes. Some of the auction guests stood staring at them outside the hotel. She glanced at her chest, noticing how the material of her gown pulled tight and held her boobs from falling out of place. It was unreal.

"Rafe, put me down!"

He laughed and spanked her ass again, the stinging turning her on at the worst moment. "No."

He started marching down the road with her on his shoulder like it wasn't a big deal. She was a big girl, and he was a giant mountain man. If they didn't call attention going down the street, nothing would.

They had just gotten to the corner when a limo pulled up beside them. He flung the door open and shoved her inside, following closely behind. There was no time to take a breath. The vehicle took off so fast she slid down the leather to the other end of the seat.

"Rafe, let me out of this car."

"I already said no."

She hated that he was putting her in this position. She loved Rafe. For the entire time they'd been together, their only issue had been his being emotionally closed off.

"Let me out now. Talking isn't going to make a difference. You should know that. You are the reason things went the way they did," she huffed, still trying to catch her breath.

He glanced at his watch. "You're going to listen to me. Whatever you decide after that is up to you."

"This is such bullshit. You know this is not the way to do things."

He frowned. "Then what is the way? Going to your house and talking about it? That didn't work.

Calling you? You changed your voicemail to say you weren't changing your mind."

She had. She'd been set on not accepting less than what she knew he could give. She didn't even care that others who called didn't understand her message. He understood. The limo slowed down. She glanced out the window and noticed they were entering the airport.

"You need to let me go. You didn't want to love me. I understand that now."

His features turned dark with anger. "You don't understand anything."

The door opened, and he got out. He leaned in to glance at her. "Come with me, Julie. If you try to run again, I'll just throw you on my shoulder and carry you, consequences be damned."

He was insane. He had to have lost his mind in the time they'd been broken up. Why else would he be so adamant about this? About her going with him? Something about how set he was on her coming with him made her stop and think. A small voice yelled inside her brain to go with him, to see what it was that could have pushed him to run away from her.

She left the limo, and he led her to a waiting private jet. She swallowed at the knot in her throat. Too many emotions clogged up her airways.

Rafe stopped at the foot of the jet and cupped her face in his hands. "Trust me. You need this. We both do."

She nodded, her heart fluttering from nerves, fear, and excitement. This was Rafe—the man she loved beyond all reason. He wanted to take her somewhere and hopefully open up to her.

The inside of the jet was sumptuous. Giant seats that reclined into beds faced forward in sets. There was a door at the back, which she assumed was the bathroom.

She didn't say anything else while they moved to takeoff position. She gulped and glanced at the man sitting beside her.

His blue eyes shone with that flash of determination and desire that made her knees weak. "I kept telling myself you wouldn't have the same effect on me this time around." He laughed, dryly. "I was wrong."

She blinked. "Wrong how?"

He leaned into her, sliding a hand into her hair and pulling her face to his. "I still want you. I want you just as much as I've wanted you every fucking second since I met you."

FIVE

She didn't get a chance to say anything. He meshed their lips together into a toe-curling kiss she couldn't have stopped if she tried. Her brain froze. She didn't know what to think. Yes, she wanted Rafe. She loved him. He was the one who didn't seem to know how to handle loving her.

She gripped his tux jacket, curling her nails tight on the material and moaning into the kiss. Her body wound tight. She struggled to get oxygen into her lungs. He didn't let up. He rubbed his tongue over hers, sending electric heat down to her pussy.

He cupped her breast over the dress, his thumb rubbing over the thin material holding her bound. Her nipples pebbled tight. She ached from how badly she wanted him. Her heart constricted with love and pain. She'd missed him so damn much. Every kiss. Every touch. Every damn thing about Rafe.

The kiss deepened. With just a growl, he turned up the heat. Her body shivered from the rampant desire coursing through her. She bit on his lip, loving the sound of his groan. His hand on her breast squeezed, kneading at her chest and caressing down to her belly. She didn't give a fuck that she didn't have flat abs or that her belly was soft and jiggly. She had rolls. She had thick thighs and large legs. She even had chubby arms. None of that mattered.

She firmly believed she was a good-looking, curvy woman, and Rafe had always made her feel like she was the hottest woman in the world. He lifted her skirt and slid his hand under the soft material, gliding a hand up her large thigh. She spread her legs open, waiting for a single touch of his hand on her sex. That's all she needed, and she'd lose it. He didn't push the panties to the side and shove a finger into her cunt like she wanted. No. He grazed his finger over her throbbing sex and continued to kiss her like the world was ending and he needed one more taste of her.

She moaned, shoving the jacket to the side and feeling the muscles underneath. The shirt had to go. In fact, all of it had to go. She'd never wanted him naked like she did that very moment.

He pulled back and gasped for air. Glancing around the cabin, she realized they were up in the air. The seat belt sign had gone off. Her pussy slickened at the all-too-possessive look he gave her.

"You…," she gasped, "…did all that to stop my nerves?"

He shook his head and took a harsh breath. "I'm not that fucking nice, princess. I did that because I haven't had a taste of you in too long, and I couldn't control the bear any longer."

Well, that was something.

She unbuckled the belt and stood. "You asked me to listen, and I will, but don't play yourself. I'm not here to be a piece of ass!"

She marched down the walkway to the back door, expecting to find a bathroom. Instead of a bathroom, what she found was a bedroom with a full bed and sheets of a higher thread count than she owned at home. And she had a thing for expensive sheets.

The door opened behind her, and she turned to face Rafe.

"You have such a strange view of reality," he said, crowding her. "Since when have you ever been 'just a piece of ass'?"

She stumbled back. The anger in his face didn't make her nervous; it excited her. She almost whimpered at how turned on she got. "I—"

He came closer and closer, until the back of her legs hit the bed. "You what, princess? Do you think that after all this time, I would go through all this trouble for sex?"

She gulped. The side of her that couldn't stay quiet reared its head. "I wouldn't know. You definitely weren't in it for love the last time I checked!"

He grabbed the back of her gown and yanked her forward, her body slamming up against his much harder one. Breaths rushed out of her lungs, and desire bloomed bright in her chest. She shouldn't be thinking of sex, but she was. She wanted him oh-so bad, like the addicted needed a fix. That's how she felt. Her hopes of being able to resist him dwindled down to nothing. Now her sole purpose was to get him worked up enough to argue with her. At least that would make her feel better.

He grabbed a fistful of her hair and yanked her head back, bringing his mouth down over hers. The plane shook, sending them both falling onto the bed with her beneath him. She fought at first, pushing and shoving him from her. Then, her brain started working against her, urging her to get him closer.

Clothes tore off, and soon she was lying there naked, his gaze roaming over her body with indescribable need. He cupped her breast and bit down on her nipple. She moaned, and her pussy turned instantly slick from his bite.

"Rafe!"

He lifted his head, his bright eyes eating her up. "That's it. I missed that: that little hitch in your voice when you're wet."

"You're insane." She gulped. "I don't do anything like that."

He gave her a grin that spoke volumes. It called her a liar. "Really?" He pushed her large thighs apart and took a deep breath. "Tell me I can't fucking smell how wet I made you from a single kiss."

She pressed her lips together and inhaled slowly. "That bear of yours has a wild imagination."

He got on his knees on the bed and yanked at the bow tie. Then she stared as he tugged on the pristine white shirt and sent buttons flying, leaving his slightly hairy chest exposed. He reached for his belt, undid it, and then moved to the button holding his pants closed. He glanced down at his fingers and slowed his movement.

She hadn't realized she was staring with her jaw hanging open. He wasn't one of those super muscular guys that had veins popping out of his body. No, what he had was a giant body with strong limbs, washboard abs, and those lines that defined his abs and pointed south that made women beyond stupid. Yeah, he had all that.

"I don't think my bear has a wild imagination. I think what I have is a woman who is still refusing to admit she's missed having me inside her."

She shook her head. "I can admit anything."

He lowered the zipper slowly, watching her the entire time. "Admit it then. Tell me you've missed having me fuck you."

SIX

His pants fluttered down, and his cock sprang free. Her throat went bone-dry, and she didn't know what the hell he'd just said. "I won't. I can live without sex. I have for a year."

She turned to face away from him, but was surprised when he sprawled himself over her, stopping her with his body and letting her feel his hardness.

"You continue to lie, princess."

"I've never lied to you."

"You are now." He grinned. "Don't you think I can tell you want me just as bad, if not worse, than you did last year?"

She tried to shake her head, but he held her face immobile. "Don't deny it. You crave me, just like I can't fucking breathe without imagining driving my cock into you. I can't think without a random image of your sexy-as-hell curves making my thoughts derail." He groaned, rocking his hips between her thighs, and liquid heat flowed from her pussy, sliding down to her ass. "I haven't slept from missing you in my arms. In my bed."

That's how she felt. Every word out of his lips reflected how she'd been living for the past year. She'd missed him so much she'd barely slept for a month. And his face was always popping into her thoughts, her day.

She slid her fingers into his hair and raked her nails over his scalp, pulling him down until their lips pressed together. The kiss was a new definition of need. Passion fired up her blood and shot lust coursing through her. She sucked on his lip and his tongue, nipping and licking and giving all she had.

He held her face still, keeping her from moving but at the same time being the aggressor she loved. She bit and scratched at him, a reaction she'd never been able to control. He had that effect on her. His grunts only made her wilder. She scored her nails down his arms and back. He pressed into her, the head of his cock slipping between her pussy lips and finding his way home into her sex.

"God, yes!" she screamed.

Tilting her hips, she wiggled to allow him better entrance and encourage him to move.

"Ah, baby. You want me."

What the fuck did he need, smoke signals? "Yes. Fuck. Me. Now."

He nipped on her chin, gliding his tongue up her jaw and down to her neck. "You taste so fucking delicious. Sweet. Salty. Sexy."

"Rafe, stop being an asshole and fuck me already."

He chuckled at her angry words. "Whatever happened to 'romance me'?"

"Fuck romance. Take me. You brought me here, and you have your dick at a spot that's making me ready to scream. You think I'm thinking of romance? Move. Now."

He pushed forward at that moment, filling her so completely that she groaned out a long breath. "Jesus, princess. You feel better than I remember."

She wiggled under him. "Rafe—"

He jerked back and drove hard, pressing her body deep into the bed. She widened her legs, needing a deeper connection with him. Hunger snapped at her core, seizing her focus. Him. Her. That's all there was. A slip and slide of his body over hers, driving the tension higher and higher.

"Fuck, baby. I can't believe it's been so long since I had you."

She bit her lip, pushing back the emotions tugging at her heart. It took a full damn year for him to realize that he couldn't live without her. "I wasn't a necessity."

He stopped mid-drive and glanced into her eyes. "Don't say that. You're more important than anyone else."

She dug her nails into the curve of his ass, drawing his body deeper. A low groan purred from her throat. The plane dipped and shook, adding new vibrations to their movements. "I learned that when it comes to you, I might be good enough to fuck, but not good enough to love."

He drove deep at an almost punishing pace, his body slamming repeatedly into hers. She held on to him, unable to do more than grab a slight breath every few seconds. The passion inside threatened to break free, cracking the tension building at her core.

"I'd fucking die for you!" he huffed, anger coating his words.

"I don't want you to die, you asshole!" she snapped.

His head dropped, and a new kiss consumed them. Fire blazed between their lips. She gave up any attempt at breathing and sucked air from his lungs. Desire pounded at her chest, and the love she'd been afraid to re-acknowledge made itself known. She couldn't ignore the fact that this was the man she'd cried months for. He was the one she had opened herself up to. Fuck all the money he had. She loved the stupid jerk with all his flaws.

He sucked on her bottom lip, biting down on her mouth and then growling by her neck. His cock plunged deeper and deeper. She gasped and groaned, her body silently begging for more.

"I fucking did everything I could to show you I care!" He bit down on her chest, hard. His tongue circled her nipple, and electric shudders raced down to her clit.

"You," she groaned. "Didn't."

Her belly trembled with every thrust. Her pussy clutched at his cock, holding him tight against her walls. Tension snapped inside her. Pleasure bathed over her in cool waves of bliss. She gasped multiple breaths, trying to get her lungs to work.

Her pussy contracted around his cock, jerking him hard. His perspiration-slick back tensed. His head lifted from her breast and dropped into the curve of her neck. Every thrust he made turned shallow and jerky, until he didn't move anymore. Her body continued riding her tidal wave of joy when he breathed into her hair, gripping the strands hard in his fists.

"Ah, princess. I've been dying to come inside you," he said, filling her body with his semen. A hot shudder raced up her back. She loved seeing him lose his tight rein on the control he loved to wield when he came. There was nothing he could do about that.

He flipped them over on the bed so she lay motionless on top of him while they both tried to regain their breathing. She hated how much she wanted to cry. She'd willingly given herself to him from the beginning, and he still continued to hold back. He couldn't even say that he loved her.

"Why?" she asked.

She knew her question might not get the response she needed, but after all this time, all the things they'd done together, she felt he owed her the truth.

"I don't understand what it is you want from me, Julie. I've shown you every way I can that I care."

She sucked in a breath. "I don't want you to tell me you care, because that's what I want." She lifted her head up from his chest and met his gaze. "I need to know what you feel. Why is it so hard for you to say those things to me?"

He glanced away from her and then went back to looking at her face. "I have always been different than the others. More internal."

She nodded. "I can understand that. You know I can. I never said I loved you, because I wanted you to say it back. When you push me for a commitment but aren't willing to admit to how you feel, that's not going to get us anywhere. I can't do things on your schedule, and I don't expect the same."

"I want to be with you. Nobody but you."

She lifted her lips in a slow grin. "That's a start, but not for marriage." She knew she was pushing him a lot more this time around, but it was because she wasn't going to go through the same thing with him again.

SEVEN

Rafe watched Julie put on one his shirts and sit on the bed cross-legged.

"You don't plan on eating?" she asked, picking up a croissant from the tray the flight attendant had brought their way. "You know you love these."

He nodded. "I'll eat something later."

The truth was that her words had done things to his insides nothing ever had. Fear and panic combined inside him. He couldn't lose her again. He wouldn't. But that meant he had to finally figure out how to tell her about his past. He'd known that buying her at the auction would mean she was going to want to know more about why he was the way he was. He hated to tell her those things, but he'd do it if it meant not losing her.

"I can see something's on your mind." She wiped her hands on a napkin and picked up the coffee cup from the tray. "Talk."

Julie had been like that—straight forward and to the point since the first day. She'd told him she'd be his on a whim, offering herself as long as he made her time in his bed worthwhile. Days turned to months, and the lust between them was more than he could handle. The bear inside him griped, snarling that she was his mate. Rafe ignored him. For months, he refused to acknowledge how special she'd become to him, how much he loved being with her.

"I once thought I met my mate," he said. The words dragged from his throat with the weight of a bulldozer.

She raised her brows and leaned back on the pillows. "You thought?"

He sensed the curiosity and concern in her. The bear wanted closer to her, but he pulled back. This wasn't the time for emotional crap. He needed to let her see why he was the way he was.

"I was young, thought she meant it when she said she loved me."

She frowned, forming her lips into an O. "I thought you shifters could detect lies?"

He laughed. "We can, but if the person believes they're telling the truth then it's the truth."

She blinked. "Wait a minute. This is like a lie detector. If you believe something then it happened?"

He nodded. "She swore up and down that I was the only man she loved. Wanted to get married and have babies. Hell, she said she wanted to be at home and take care of children. That it was her purpose in life."

She raised her brows and snorted. "It wasn't?"

"Not only that, apparently she was running the same story to a few other shifters."

She gasped. "No way! How did you figure it out?"

He curled his hands into fists. "It was hard at first, because I didn't see her for weeks at a time due to work. Then, I didn't see her because of her own schedule. When I finally did see her, I scented something different in her."

Julie's eyes turned saucer wide. "Was she pregnant?"

He shook his head. The memory hit him in the gut like a ton of bricks. "She'd mated someone else. The guy's scent was all over her."

"Ouch! What did she say?"

He gave a cynical laugh. "She had the nerve to continue trying to feed me the line about still loving me. Love. For a long time I didn't want to hear the word. It brought me nothing but problems."

She put her mug down softly. "Is it hard for you to believe when someone tells you they love you?"

This was the part he'd hated admitting. Emotions weren't his strong suit. He knew he wanted Julie. Hell, he'd been ready to marry and spend the rest of his life with her, but he didn't know how to deal with the love word. "I prefer to deal with actions."

She pursed her lips and nodded. "I can understand that. With that kind of experience, I would have a hard time believing anything anyone said too."

A rush of relief poured through him. Thank goodness she understood. Maybe now they could move past this love issue and focus on mating.

"It's sad," she sighed. "Being able to admit your feelings to yourself is so liberating." She met his gaze and glanced down at his naked chest. Leaning forward, she placed a hand over his heart, her lips tipping down in sadness. "You deserve to feel, Rafe. I know how I feel about you. I've never hidden it. I love you. And if the word love is what bothers you, then I'll put it to you this way: I knew that you and I would be together again, because my life is empty if you're not in it."

Sweet happiness curled around his heart. He felt the same. He'd known that she was the only person he'd ever be happy with. The bear inside him knew she was the one for them too. He'd been pushing Rafe to find Julie again and claim her in their primal way, as well as the human way. He wanted her in every way possible.

"Mr. Sinclair," the pilot spoke over the intercom. "We'll be landing shortly. Please return to your seats and buckle up. We have some strong winds and would like to make sure we bring you safely to the ground."

"Plan on telling me where the heck we're going now?" she asked with a smile.

"You'll find out soon enough."

EIGHT

Vegas. He'd taken her to Sin City. The smile on Julie's face grew with every step they took toward the waiting limo. She couldn't even find it in her to be embarrassed that she wore a man's dress shirt as an outfit. She had no shame.

The lights and sounds of Las Vegas lit up an internal flame in her. She'd always loved that city. It was one of the places she and Rafe had always talked about visiting together. She stared out the window, her face pressed against the limo glass like a kid in a toy store. One of her favorite things about Vegas was the shows. She wasn't much of a gambler, but the shows were fun and kept her highly entertained.

"You brought me to Vegas for what?" she finally asked.

Rafe continued to stare at her with a secretive smile that made her wonder what he was up to.

"You look like you need a break."

"And my job?"

He shrugged. "I spoke to your director. He's a friend."

She blinked her eyes wide. "You mean to tell me you asked for time off for me?"

He nodded and grabbed her hand, hauling her onto his lap. "Yeah."

"What if I hadn't agreed to go with you?"

Another shrug. He acted like he didn't have a care in the world, but his eyes spoke differently. His hands, curled around her waist, held her in a cage of tension. "I would have abducted you."

"Um, that's kind of what you did."

He shook his head, his lips tipping up in a gorgeous grin. "Then that answers your question. No matter how you look at it, you were coming here with me."

"You're so full of yourself!"

She turned her face away from him. A whisper of a breath blew by her neck. "Look at me, Julie."

She gulped at the flutters in her belly and faced him. The impact of those deep-blue eyes didn't go unnoticed. She felt hot and cold at the same time. "Yes?"

"Let's cut the bullshit."

She twisted in his grasp, turning to face him at a better angle. "Please, go on. I'm very interested to know what your next words are going to be."

"I fucking love you, Julie!"

Her heart thundered hard in her chest, robbing her of the ability to breathe, much less speak. She watching his face tighten with pain.

"I—"

"No. Don't say anything. Just listen." He slipped his hands around her head, cradling her face between his palms. "You don't know how hard it's been to be without you, knowing that I can't sleep much less be at peace when you're far from me. It's been killing me slowly. Your absence has destroyed every happiness I had for my job and the world. I don't like you being away from me." His brows dipped in a ferocious frown. "And I don't like knowing you are unhappy either." He glanced down at her lips then back at her eyes, the hot look sending shivers down her spine. "You and I, we belong together. Same species or not. We fucking belong to each other. I don't give a fuck what the world or society thinks. You are mine."

He was right. They both knew it. She leaned forward, bringing her lips to his and offering them for his ownership. Sweet joy spread through her, pulling a soft sigh of surrender from her lips. It was time to move on from all the things that she knew held them back, including her expectations. She loved him. She'd happily take him back if he took things slow.

He kissed her softly, not the usual aggressive, desperate bear in need to take her type of kiss. It was a kiss that spoke of all the feelings she'd never heard him say.

The limo stopped, and the door opened. He helped her out of the vehicle. Her legs were still wobbly from the earth-shattering kiss.

She glanced up and was floored by the location. She met his gaze and then looked down at her outfit. She had his shirt on. His shirt! As a dress.

"Tell me this is a joke," she mumbled. Her brain had stopped working the moment she saw the sign for the "Little Chapel of Love" blinking in front of them.

"It's not a joke, Julie." He grabbed her arms and made her face him. "I love you. I'm willing to admit that and do anything I need to for us to have the relationship we want." He got down on one knee, leaving her completely speechless. "Will you marry me?"

"Right now?" she squeaked. "Wearing your shirt?"

A smile flirted over his lips and a twinkle lit in his eyes. "Yes. Now. I don't care what you wear.

You're always going to be the most beautiful woman in the world to me. With or without clothes."

How could she say no to him when he said things like that?

"This is crazy."

"Say yes, already!" said a group of old women passing them by.

She nodded, the words stuck in the back of her throat. "Okay."

"Okay?"

Tears clogged her throat, making it nearly impossible to speak. "Yes. I'll marry you."

He swooped her up in his arms, twirling her like she weighed next to nothing, and then put her back down on her feet. "I love you."

She flung her arms around his neck and kissed him. This time, she was the aggressor. She drove her tongue into his mouth. She moaned when he groaned, and sucked on his lips. All sense of propriety gone, she didn't give a shit who saw them standing in the middle of a busy sidewalk, making out while she wore next to nothing.

He pulled back from the kiss, his breath coming out in short bursts like hers. "Come on, beautiful. I'm never letting you go again."

The chapel was small and decorated nicely for a small ceremony. She walked in, and a man in a suit stood by the front of the pews.

She glanced up at Rafe with a grin. "What? No Elvis?"

He shook his head. "I said we'd get married. I didn't say it had to be crazy."

She giggled. The entire thing was crazy. She had on sexy sandals with a man's shirt for a dress, her hair all over the place from having sex with Rafe on the jet, and her makeup probably smeared to hell. Did she care? Nope. She felt as nervous and excited as any woman on her wedding day.

An older woman appeared by her side out of nowhere, handing her a bouquet of fake flowers and trying to pass her a veil. She took the flowers but declined the veil. There was no way that was going to help out her outfit.

Music played, and they walked up the aisle hand in hand. This was no traditional wedding. This was them finally having their chance to be happy.

She gasped when he pulled a box out of his pocket when the minister asked for rings. Her eyes filled with tears, and a happy smile covered her face. "You really thought this through, huh?"

He shook his head. "Not even a little. I've had these for you since before you left. There was going to be no other woman to take your place in my life. Ever."

Once they exchanged vows, they kissed, and the world was once again a perfect place.

NINE

"You're going to break your back, you silly bear!" She laughed, her head swimming from all the champagne they'd had in the limo. He didn't bother putting her down, though. Instead, he pressed a kiss to her neck and licked, sending fire down to her belly.

"Open the door, and let's get you naked."

She giggled and shook her head. "You are such a romantic, Mr. Sinclair."

"I might be, but you're my inspiration, Mrs. Sinclair."

She had never seem him smiling so openly, like he didn't have a single care in the world. Her heart felt light. She'd never felt this emotionally connected to Rafe. Not even in the past.

She opened the door to their suite, and once they were inside, he kicked it closed with his foot.

The room was gorgeous: all glass that overlooked the strip. She knew there was no better view in the entire hotel. He'd made sure to get it for them. Her interest wasn't the view. It was the smile of joy on Rafe's face.

"I can't believe we did it."

He carried her all the way to the bedroom and placed her gently on the bed. Before she got chance to scoot back, he tugged the high heels off her feet and started to undress.

"I believe it," he said, hunkering down on the bed and pushing her legs open to stare at her bare sex. "You've been walking around without any panties?"

She laughed. "What did you expect? You broke mine!"

He dropped down to his knees and pressed his face between her legs, rubbing his cheek on her inner thigh. "I fucking love your scent. A combo of you and me. That's how it's always going to be."

She unbuttoned the shirt, letting it fall off her shoulders and holding herself up on her elbows. "Lick my pussy, Rafe."

He swept his tongue over her pussy lips, spreading them open and then gliding down to her entrance. "*Ahh.* You taste even better now than before. I can taste myself on you. Fucking delicious."

Her belly clenched hard, and her pussy grasped at the nothingness of being unfulfilled. She needed him so bad. He licked up and down her folds, sucking and groaning on her flesh. Her muscles tightened with amazing speed. If she weren't so turned on, she'd wonder how the hell he got her this close to orgasm so quickly.

He flicked his tongue around her clit in circles. Her breaths came in short, harsh bursts. It got harder and harder to breathe. She clutched at the sheets, her body unraveling. Pleasure washed over her in satisfying waves. She felt her body loosen as her orgasm rocked through her.

Before she got a chance to catch her breath, he flipped her on her stomach, straddling her legs. She lay flat, wondering why he didn't raise her ass into a doggy-style position. Her question was answered when he pushed her legs open and pressed his cock into her. He then leaned over her, his chest grazing her back, and moved her hands to either side of her.

"Hold on," he whispered by her ear.

She fisted the sheet and waited. The heat of his body enveloped them. Passion rose with her temperature, turning her skin hot and slick with sweat. She wiggled under him only to have him grab her by the neck and pin her down, pushing his cock in and out of her hard and fast.

"Rafe," she moaned.

"I told you to hold on," he groaned.

She hadn't realized this position would have the impact it did. She couldn't touch him, and he took her over and over again without allowing her to move. Every second he drove deep and pulled back, pressing her into the mattress with the weight of his hips. He licked the back of her shoulder, biting his way up to her earlobe.

"Fuck! You're so damn tight. I can't believe how much I missed being inside you."

She tried to look over her shoulder, but his hand on her neck kept her in place.

"I missed you inside me too," she choked out.

He fucked her fast and deep. The strength of his strokes left her barely able to breathe, much less speak. She squeezed the sheets in her grasp, wishing it were his body she touched.

"I'm never letting you go."

The possessive tone lit desperation in her chest. Her love for him expanded at the thought of his words.

"I don't want to be let go. Hold on to me, Rafe."

"You're mine," he grunted. "Fucking mine. My wife. My mate. There's no other woman I'd give my last breath for."

With every word he spoke, he fucked her harder, until he was driving deep and pulling back to do it again.

"I love you," she moaned, her body ready to explode from the impending climax.

"Jesus," he breathed, biting her neck. "I can't get enough of you."

That was it. The looming edge rushed toward her, and her body broke as pleasure swelled and took her over.

"Oh, god!" she screamed, her body going stiff for a second before loosening up.

He pounded her hard. Harder. Deeper. And stopped suddenly, his body shaking at her back and his cock pulsing inside her, filling her with his cum.

"That's it, baby. Take my fucking cum. I love how your pussy squeezes hard," he said. "Suck my dick with your pussy, sweetheart. Let my seed grow inside you. You're mine. I'm never letting you go."

He slid off her body and lay next to her, rearranging her so that she lay with her leg draped over his and her body cushioned on his side.

It took a long moment of hard breathing before the world settled and she could speak.

She glanced up at his face. "You really mean that?"

"I'm never letting you go. I love you."

She smiled, her heart bursting with joy. "I know. That's not what I meant though."

He caressed a hand over her lips, a ghost of a smile curving over his. "Yes. I want you pregnant with my child. You're the only woman I have ever said that to. I'm not an emotional talker, but for you, I'll try. I will try my damnedest for you. At everything."

She couldn't ask for more. A fresh start with her bear was exactly what they needed.

SIGN UP FOR MILLY'S NEWSLETTER FOR LATEST NEWS!

http://eepurl.com/pt9q1

Find out more about Milly Taiden here:
Email: millytaiden@gmail.com
Website: http://www.millytaiden.com
Facebook: http://www.facebook.com/
millytaidenpage
Twitter: https://www.twitter.com/millytaiden

ALSO BY MILLY TAIDEN

Sassy Mates Series
Scent of a Mate *Sassy Mates Book One*
A Mate's Bite *Sassy Mates Book Two*
Unexpectedly Mated *Sassy Mates Book Three*
A Sassy Wedding *Short 3.7*
The Mate Challenge *Sassy Mates Book Four*
Sassy in Diapers *Short 4.3*

Federal Paranormal Unit
Wolf Protector *Federal Paranormal Unit Book One*
Dangerous Protector *Federal Paranormal Unit Book Two*

Black Meadow Pack
Sharp Change *Black Meadows Pack Book One*
Caged Heat *Black Meadows Pack Book Two*

Paranormal Dating Agency
Twice the Growl *Book One*
Geek Bearing Gifts *Book Two*
The Purrfect Match *Book Three*
Curves 'Em Right *Book Four*
Tall, Dark and Panther *Book Five*
The Alion King *Book Six*

FUR-ocious Lust - Bears
Fur-Bidden *Book One*

Fur-Gotten *Book Two*
Fur-Given Book *Three*

FUR-ocious Lust - Tigers
Stripe-Tease *Book Four*
Stripe-Search *Book Five*
Stripe-Club *Book Six*

Other Works
Wolf Fever
Fate's Wish
Wynter's Captive
Sinfully Naughty Vol. 1
Club Duo Boxed Set
Don't Drink and Hex
Hex Gone Wild
Hex and Kisses
Hex You Up *(coming soon)*
Hex with an Ex *(coming soon)*
Alpha Owned
Bitten by Night
Seduced by Days
Mated by Night
Taken by Night
Captured by Night *(coming soon)*
Match Made in Hell
Hellhound Needs a Mate *(coming soon)*

About the Author

New York Times and USA Today Bestselling Author Milly Taiden (AKA April Angel) loves to write sexy stories. How sexy? So sexy they will surely make your e-reader sizzle. Usually paranormal or contemporary, her stories are a great, quick way to satisfy your craving for fun heroines with curves and sexy alphas with fur.

Milly lives in New York City with her hubby, their boy child, and their little dog "Needy Speedy." She's aware she's bossy and is addicted to shoe shopping, chocolate (but who isn't, right?), and Dunkin' Donuts coffee.

She loves to meet new readers!

Made in the USA
Charleston, SC
13 September 2016